Just as You Are

MINDY BURBIDGE STRUNK

Chapter One

Hanora Pemberton stepped into the breakfast room and nearly stepped back out again. Something was amiss. She could feel it. And the pointed look her mother gave her only confirmed her suspicions.

Her father looked up and smiled. "Ah, Nora. Please, sit down. I've a surprise for you."

Nora's stomach twisted into knots, and she lifted a hand to the curl hanging at the side of her cheek. Were not surprises to be anticipated, rather than dreaded? She sat in the chair the footman held out but remained stiff-backed and wary.

Her mother cast her a nervous smile. Gads, that could not be good.

"I've decided it is time to present you at court and give you a Season." Her father gave her a pleased smile.

The air hissed from Nora's lips, and she cast a wide-eyed glance at her mother. Surely she had heard him wrong. A Season? That could not have been what he said. "I beg your pardon?" She pulled her mobcap down closer to her face.

Her father, who usually narrowed his eyes at the deplorable thing, offered her a soft smile. Why had he not commented on it as he had every other time?

The chair creaked as he leaned back and ran his hand over his slightly protruding belly. "A Season, Nora. After all these years, it is your turn." His normally boisterous voice quieted.

Nora swallowed, reaching again for the curl. "But Papa, I'm two and twenty. I'm too old."

Her father batted away her words. "Nonsense."

Nora twisted the tips of her fingers. "It's too soon. Agatha isn't yet married." She bit down on her lip. Her excuses sounded reasonable, did they not?

"She will be by week's end. There is no reason to wait another year to present you at court." He frowned. "I had thought you would be excited. You have been begging for years to have a Season." He eyed her closely and her skin itched. Did he know?

"I'm thrilled, Papa." There was little excitement in her tone. "But I'm just concerned. What if something should happen and the wedding doesn't take place?" She turned desperate eyes on her mother.

"Dearest," her mother chided softly. "Please do not tempt the fates. Your sister's wedding will happen as planned, and we will go to London." A stranger may have taken the words as a scolding, but Nora knew her mother didn't mean it.

"It all seems so rushed. Next year Agatha will be settled and the expense of her marriage will not be felt so keenly." Appealing to her father's financial sense would surely change his mind.

"The only wedding expense is that of the wedding clothes your mother insists Agatha must have. But it isn't so much as to prohibit you from having your Season." He studied her again. "You're a handsome enough girl, Nora, but there is no guarantee you'll secure a match in your first Season. And if we wait another year, it only puts the time off for your younger sisters to have their turn."

"But—"

He clicked his tongue. "You let me worry about the finances. We leave for London in a fortnight." He glanced at Nora's younger sister. "You too, Lizzie. You'll not yet be out, but you may visit the sights with your sister."

Lizzie fidgeted on the other side of the table, her eyes dancing with excitement. "Thank you, Papa."

Nora closed her eyes and rubbed at her temple. "Thank you, Papa." Never had the words felt so hollow. She stood, ignoring the breakfast she'd not tasted. "I feel a headache coming on. I best return to my chambers."

Her mother looked up. Worry etched new lines on her face. Had Nora caused them? "I'll be along shortly to check on you, dearest."

Nora hurried up the stairs to her chambers. She closed the door softly behind her and moved over to the window seat. Dropping her head against the pane, she stared out at the dry, stubbled fields. While Nora could not see the razor-sharp shafts from this distance, she knew they were there, ready to leave a nasty cut on an unsuspecting intruder.

But their cut could not possibly hurt as bad as the pain in her stomach. How could Papa make them go to London? That was the last place she wished to be. If he had only taken her when she was in her prime, when she'd asked all those times, everything would be different. But Papa was nothing if not proper. And a younger daughter could not be out before the older one was married.

A quiet knock sounded at the door, and she glanced over to see her father peering into the room. He stepped inside and cleared his throat. "Your mother explained your reluctance to me when I mentioned my plans to her last night."

Nora looked down at the floor. She could imagine the disgust and disappointment she would surely see in his eyes. That must have been why he had studied her so closely at breakfast. He was trying to see just how bad it was.

"I'm sorry, Papa. I've tried everything I can think of to grow the hair back. But nothing works." She bit hard on her cheek to keep her emotions in check. Tears would not help. "Surely you see why I can't go to London. It would be a disaster."

She didn't see or hear him come closer, but the air seemed to move out of his way, lifting the hairs on her arms ever so slightly.

"I see nothing of the sort. The revelation did nothing to change my mind." He put an awkward hand on her shoulder. "You need this Season, Nora. You need to secure a match now more than ever."

Nora looked up at last, and the tears she'd kept at bay finally spilled over her lids. Not because of what she saw in her father's gaze, but because of what was absent. There was no disgust or disappointment, only a look of concern. And perhaps even a bit of pain. "If that is what you wish, Papa."

He lifted his hand from her shoulder, but not before giving her a gentle squeeze. "It will all work out for the best, Nora. Of that I'm certain."

"I wish I felt such confidence."

He smiled and winked at her. "Perhaps you just need to borrow a bit of mine."

Another knock sounded, and they both looked to see her mother standing in the doorway.

"I'll leave you to your mother." Her father smiled fondly at his wife before closing the door behind him.

Her mother motioned to the window seat, and they both sat down.

Nora leaned into her mother's arm and sighed. "What are we to do, Mama? Papa is determined. But you and I both know that London is the last place I should be."

Her mother sighed. "Yes, he's quite determined."

"Can you not change his mind?"

Her mother shook her head. "Your father and I spoke at length last evening, and we agree that perhaps this isn't so very bad. I believe we can make this work to our advantage."

Nora snorted. "Mama, how can this possibly work to our

advantage?" She pulled at the mobcap, revealing her nearly completely bald head.

Her mother sighed, then covered it with a cough. "Oh, dearest, it is worse than the last time I saw it."

Nora ran her hand over her scalp. She wrapped a slight curl—the small patch of hair remaining—around her finger. "It has been constant for the last month, Mama. I'm afraid by the time we reach London, even this will not remain." She lifted the curl, and then let it fall back to her face.

The bedroom door burst open and Lizzie hurried in. "Nora, Nora. Is it not exciting? Papa has agreed to take us both to London." She clasped her hands together, a wistful look on her face. "Perhaps next year will be my—." Her eyes widened as she stared at Nora's bald head. "No—Nora. What happened to your hair?"

Nora yanked the mobcap back into place. Why could Lizzie never knock? And why did both her mother and sister look at her with looks of pity and shock? The pain in her stomach deepened, and her hand dropped from her cap into her lap. Her shoulders drooped. "It started nearly 6 months ago."

Lizzie stepped forward and reached out a hand, gently touching the hair at Nora's temple. "Six months? Why have you not told me of this?" She swallowed. "Did you not trust me to keep your secret?"

"Now isn't the time to discuss it. Your sister and I have plans we need to discuss. Please return to your room." Her mother shooed Lizzie away.

"But I can help." Lizzie gave one last look at Nora before she nodded and slipped from the room.

Nora stared at the door long after it closed. Finally, she stood up and walked toward the fireplace. "I know you think there is a way to make this Season successful, but we both know if anyone should find out about my hair..."

"It is a risk, I admit." Her mother lifted a shoulder. "We shall simply have to ensure that no one finds out."

Nora's eyes widened. "And how do you suggest we do that, Mama? It isn't as if I can wear a mobcap around London. Papa barely tolerates it here. It would not be acceptable at the balls. And I cannot wear a bonnet wherever I go."

Her mother stood and pulled Nora to a stop. She wrapped her arm around Nora's waist and gave her a little squeeze. "Dearest, what do you wish for your life? What do you imagine for yourself in five years? What do you hope to be?"

"Five years?" Nora looked down at her hands, picking at each nail. "I do not know. I once dreamed of love and marriage. But now?" She heaved a sigh. "Now I simply hope I survive London with a small amount of dignity still in place. Perhaps after the Season, I may look further into the future."

A sadness fell over her mother's features. "I miss the girl who wished for love. She was spontaneous and delightful."

The corner of Nora's lips turned. "And troublesome."

Her mother grinned. "Perhaps I do not miss that part. But I do miss your confidence and optimism."

Nora swallowed down the tears threatening again. "There is little to be confident or optimistic about anymore, Mama."

Her mother released her and folded her arms across her chest. "I disagree. I do not believe your dreams must change simply because of your situation."

"Situation?" Nora snorted. "It isn't as if my hair changed color, Mama. It is gone."

"Perhaps not completely." Her mother tapped her finger to her lips. "I know of a very fine wig maker. My mother frequented him often when we were in London when I was a girl."

Nora's maid entered from the adjoining dressing room. "Oh, a wig?" She stopped short and looked to the floor. "I beg your pardon. If I may, that seems a very fine idea. London will have the finest shops, will it not?" She hurried over to a basket at the side of Nora's dressing table. Opening the top, she removed several balls of yarn, placing them aside. She reached in and withdrew two large handfuls of blonde hair. "Do you think he might have a use for this? I've heard they sometimes use human hair to make the finest wigs. Would it not be best if he could use your own?"

"How long have you been collecting my hair, Penny?"

"Almost from the beginning. I had hoped I could use it to put more curls in your bonnets as time went on. But a wig would be a better use for it." She glanced at the basket. "There is more inside."

Nora looked from her maid to her mother before her gaze rested on the hair in Penny's hands. "But Mama, wigs aren't in fashion anymore. How do you even know your mother's wig maker is still in business? What if he has closed his shop?" She took up her pacing, rubbing at her brows with her fingertips. "Even if his shop is still there, I'm certain it would take weeks to make something of quality. We will not arrive with any time to spare."

Her mother pulled her to a stop and held her in place. "Then I suppose I shall have to convince your father to leave for London early. We can depart as soon as the wedding is over."

Nora breathed in slowly, allowing her stomach and her emotions to quiet. "Do you think Papa will agree?"

Her mother patted Nora on the arm gently and moved towards the door. "My dear, your father isn't the only determined person in this family."

Chapter Two

Nora stepped inside the doorway of her family's St. James Square townhouse as she pulled at the ribbons on her bonnet and carefully lifted it from her head. Her new wig was snug, but she felt it shift slightly when she lifted the straw bonnet off. She would grow accustomed to it, would she not? This was only the first day she'd had it.

She glanced around, hoping a footman or maid had not noticed, but thankfully, no one was about. Nora moved to the side table, set her bonnet down, and stared into the long mirror hanging above. She sucked in a breath, taken aback for a moment at the sight of hair on her head. Six months was a long time to see herself bald. And while she had not thought she'd fully grown accustomed to the sight, she now wondered if she'd been wrong.

While she could detect some differences between her former hair and the wig she now wore, her mother had insisted no one would notice. Penny had done well in saving the hair. The wigmaker had only used a small amount from elsewhere.

Nora reached up and ran a hand over the wig. Where the rest had come from, she didn't wish to know.

"It is a very fine wig, dearest. No one will know it isn't yours." Her mother whispered as she pulled her fingers from her gloves.

"But it is my real hair, Mama."

"Precisely, so stop looking so forlorn."

"I hope you had a pleasant afternoon, my lady." Their butler, Higgins, stepped up beside them and gathered the articles from the table as he waited to help them remove their pelisses.

Nora's mother finished unbuttoning hers first and turned for Higgins to help her remove it. "Indeed, Higgins, we had a splendid time."

Rumbling laughter sounded from down the corridor as Nora slowly pulled at the tips of her gloves. A smile pulled at her lips. Her father's laughter was always infectious and boisterous. And after the tedious afternoon at the wig shop and modiste, she needed something lighthearted.

Her father emerged in the entryway with a strange man at his side, and Nora's smile froze.

The man was younger than her father, but much older than Nora if the gray at his temple was any indication. His hair was longer on top, swooping up and back from his brow. But unlike his side whiskers, the rest of his hair was deep brown. The dark metal of his glasses framed his gray-blue eyes. It was an altogether pleasant sight. At an earlier time, Nora might have thought an association possible . . . even desirable.

Her father's eyes lit up when he spotted Nora and her mother. "Capital, capital. Your timing is just right, my dear." He motioned to the man at his side. "Charlotte, you remember Jeremy Fagan, do you not?"

Nora's mother's eyes widened slightly. "Captain Fagan? How long has it been? I should say at least a decade, if not more."

Lord Pemberton slapped Captain Fagan on the back. "He's no longer a captain, my dear. He is now Rear Admiral Fagan."

Her mother's mouth dropped slightly open, but she recovered quickly. "I knew you would advance far in the Navy, sir."

Nora watched the interaction through her lashes.

Admiral Fagan dipped his head, but no smile turned his lips.

"Lady Pemberton. It is a pleasure to see you again after more than *fifteen* years."

"Fifteen years? It seems like just yesterday."

Nora kept her face down but continued to watch the Admiral. She didn't recall ever meeting a Captain. And she most assuredly had never met an Admiral. How did her parents know this man?

He looked at her and dipped his head again. "Miss Hanora, your father and I were just speaking of you—"

"It is Miss Pemberton, now," her mother corrected. "Our eldest daughter is recently married." She moved over and nudged Nora closer to the gentleman.

The heat rose in Nora's cheeks. How was she to make it through this Season if her mother and father pointed her out to everyone they saw? She would never blend in with the crowds.

"Admiral Fagan's father taught me much about my role in Lords, as my own father died when I was very young. It grieved me when Lord Fagan died." Her father looked at the Admiral with obvious pride. "I was happy to do the same for his children, especially Jeremy. He's one of the best people I know."

"Admiral Fagan, it is a pleasure to meet you." She kept her gaze trained on her shoes. They were close enough now that he could likely tell she wore a wig. Her cheeks heated again.

"The Admiral is to join us for dinner this evening."

She glanced up in surprise. "He's to join us? For dinner?" Her fingers went to the curl at the side of her face but slid down until her hand rested at the nape of her neck, her mouth suddenly dry. Dinner would put them even closer together. Indeed, the Admiral would likely sit next to her at the table. Would he discover the wig? She swallowed and pasted a smile on her face. "How lovely. I shall anticipate seeing you this evening, Admiral."

The Admiral's brow creased as he dipped his head to her again. "As shall I."

Nora continued to smile, but only because it was the polite

thing to do. His face showed no more excitement about the evening than hers likely did.

~

NORA WAS NOT sure what to expect at dinner that night. Admiral Fagan had not seemed the least bit excited when her father had mentioned the invitation. And she could not imagine he was much of a conversationalist. But perhaps that was all for the best. If the evening was dull, perhaps it would end early.

She looked up from her book as Higgins announced the Admiral's arrival.

As he stepped into the parlor, she noticed his face was every bit as stern as it had been earlier that day. Nora tilted her head to the side, examining the man while his attention was elsewhere.

Perhaps stern was not the right word. He didn't look angry or mad. He simply looked . . . disinterested?

Again, just as he had earlier, he nodded his head as he greeted each person in the room.

Her mother rushed over, clasping the Admiral by the arm and guiding him over to the settee by the fire. "Admiral Fagan, I do not believe you have met my younger daughter, Elizabeth." Her mother directed her gaze to Lizzie.

Lizzie's cheeks reddened. While she longed to be out in society, she was not yet accustomed to all it entailed.

"Miss Elizabeth." The Admiral gave her the same greeting as everyone else.

"It's a pleasure, sir." Lizzie ducked behind her mother.

"Dinner is not yet served, but perhaps we could talk while we wait. Much has happened since last we saw you." Her mother motioned to a chair across from Nora, then took the seat next to him, clasping her hands at her chest. "I'm sure we would all love to hear about your time in the Navy."

The Admiral shrugged. "I'm not sure there's much of interest to say."

"Oh, that can't be true. Did you not serve in the wars against Napoleon? How could that be anything but interesting?" Her mother leaned forward slightly, opening her fan and flicking it rapidly. "I'm sure you have many tales to share."

"It is hardly dinner conversation, my lady. And not proper for the ears of such fine ladies." The Admiral looked uncomfortable. Perhaps he was not the type to relish speaking about himself and his exploits.

While Nora did not object to hearing about them, she found it refreshing that he did not share. From her experience, most men could not wait to tell the fairer sex about their feats of bravery and heroics. And the Admiral surely had some to share.

Nora looked at her father, rather than the Admiral. "Papa, have you been to the bookstore at Covent Garden? Mama and I walked past it when we were shopping for my new gowns." She and her mother shared a look. "It is so much bigger than anything we have back in Mickle."

The Admiral looked appraisingly at her, and she dropped her gaze.

Her father grinned. "Of course it is. This is London. Everything is bigger in London."

"And grander," added her mother.

Nora smiled at her parents, but she did not feel it. She looked down at her hands. Her view of London was not like her parents'. From her experience, it was bigger than Mickle, but it was also less friendly. People bustled about the streets jostling into each other with barely a pardon uttered.

"I believe I shall return to the shop and spend some time perusing its shelves. I've a little pin money saved up." She glanced over at the Admiral from the corner of her eye, hoping he would pick up on the topic without her having to address him directly. She had noticed how intently he studied people as he spoke to them. And she didn't wish to be the subject of his stare.

He straightened his glasses but remained quiet. Perhaps he was not fond of reading.

Nora tried again. "Tell me, Admiral, what brings you to London? Are you on leave?" She lifted her gaze just long enough to ask but dropped it again before he could scrutinize her. It was not the politest thing to do, but it was all she could manage.

"A bit of both. I've received a new assignment, but I'm in London for a few months until I assume my post."

She chanced a sidelong glance at him as he smiled. Or rather, his face softened. She sighed. It made him look more friendly. Someone should tell him to do it more often.

Her father leaned forward in his chair. "Ah, yes. I heard of your appointment from Sir Thomas Thompson—the Comptroller of the Navy," he added for his wife and daughter's benefit, "at White's this afternoon. It is a great opportunity for you, Jeremy. Although, I'm sure you'll miss our English society."

Nora's mother tilted her head. "You've been assigned a new ship?"

The Admiral leaned back in his seat and crossed his leg over his knee, interlacing his fingers around it. "Yes, of a sort. I'm to be a special envoy to New Zealand. There are those in the government that believe there are benefits in securing the islands for England."

Nora's mother let out a small gasp. "New Zealand? That sounds dreadful. Is it not the same as New South Wales—fully peopled with criminals?"

"No, no, not at all. The native people are the only inhabitants currently. I'm to take gifts and try to forge better relationships with the leaders, perhaps come to some sort of agreement so a colony might be possible."

Nora sat forward in her seat. "It sounds both exciting and lonely."

He darted a glance at her and she ducked her head.

"It will not be the same as England, but I'm certain it will have its own pleasures. Besides, I rather enjoy being alone." He glanced at her before looking away. Was that his way of saying he didn't enjoy their company? Or maybe just hers? Was it because of her wig?

"I cannot be as certain as you are, Admiral. I think even India would be preferable." Her mother's fan waved furiously.

"India was marvelous. I quite enjoyed my time there." The Admiral scratched at his ear. "But as I'm not one who cares for society, I find I'm looking forward to this new position. I shall have plenty of time to do as I please. Perhaps I shall finally have a moment to read."

Then he enjoyed reading. Why had he not taken up her previous conversation? Nora studied the hard features of his face. His angular jaw and slightly crooked nose—perhaps from a fight?—made him appear stern. But if she really looked, she thought she could see kindness in his eyes, although she didn't know him well enough to say for certain.

She thought back on her previous assessment and nodded to herself. No, stern had not been correct. He seemed to her to be the quiet sort—one who preferred his own company or the company of a select few over that of the masses. And while a year ago, Nora would not have understood that desire, she did now. Certainly the natives in New Zealand cared not about a lack of hair, not as London Society would if they discovered it. She mentally shook her head. What was she thinking? It was not as if she would visit New Zealand anytime soon.

The butler entered and announced dinner, and everyone stood to follow him into the dining room. The Admiral extended his arm to Nora.

She accepted it and allowed him to escort her down the corridor. When they entered the dining room, he stood to the side as the footman pulled out her chair. Then he took the seat beside her.

Nora's parents spoke in quiet tones to each other as the footman dished the food. Were they intentionally leaving them out of their conversation? Was this their way of forcing her to speak with the Admiral?

Nora looked over at him. "Are you going to miss being aboard your ship once you arrive in New Zealand?"

The Admiral put down his fork and knife and held Nora's gaze. She wanted to look away but knew better. "In the beginning, I should think I'll need to live aboard the ship while we build accommodations. Once they are complete, then living on land will likely be the most difficult part of this assignment."

"I should think after being on a ship for so long, it would be hard to stay on land for an extended period."

The Admiral stared more intently at her, and she raised a hand to her temple, but she could not pull her gaze away.

"Most people do not understand that aspect. They think I should be happy to stay on land at last. What they do not seem to understand is that the movement of the ship, the smell of the sea —they are home to me. I've lived on a ship for more years of my life than not."

"And how do you think you shall adapt?" Nora rested her utensils on the plate, looking at him. "Do you think you'll enjoy living in New Zealand?"

The Admiral pulled his gaze from hers and picked up his knife and fork.

She frowned. What had made him look away? She fingered the curl at her cheek.

"I'm excited for the challenge. It shall be unlike anything I have undertaken." He put a small bite of mutton in his mouth and chewed thoughtfully before swallowing. "It is a good opportunity. But if I find it does not suit, then I shall return to England."

"You make it sound as if returning early would be the end of your career."

"It likely would be. My advancement to Rear Admiral is based on the success of this assignment." He shrugged. "But it isn't as if I shall be in complete ruin. I have a small estate that my brother is managing in Westmorland. I can always return and take over its management." His words said he would be happy, but his face said the opposite. Would he ever be happy on land?

"Will you be done with the sea once this assignment is over?"

"I do not know." Admiral Fagan shook his head. "I do not believe I shall ever be done with the sea. My estate is on the coast. Perhaps I shall anchor a ship in her cove and live aboard it." He grinned down at his plate—the first real grin she had seen from him.

Nora stared down at her plate. "You're lucky to have options."

"Yes, I am. There are many who aren't so fortunate."

As I'm daily aware. Nora sighed.

"Shall you take a wife with you to New Zealand?" Nora's mother asked.

Nora cast an annoyed glance at her mother, but she was uncertain if it was the question or the interruption that annoyed her most. They had been having a perfectly amiable conversation before her mother's interruption.

The Admiral's brow creased for a split second before it smoothed out again. "If I should find a lady who could fill the role, then perhaps. But few ladies could live under such conditions. It will take someone special. If I find such a lady while I'm in London, then I suppose I shall make her an offer."

"If you find a wife, you are to take her with you? Is there not danger involved?" Nora's mother pressed.

"Perhaps a little. But my assignment is to make peace with the natives. I'm to win their trust and friendship. I believe the right wife could help with such measures. Besides, I do not wish to marry just to leave her behind. It is why I must be certain I have found the right one." He flicked a glance at Nora.

"If you aren't intent on finding a wife, what do you hope to accomplish while in London?" Her father asked.

"I'm to be away for several years—two, at least. I hope to see a play or visit a museum. But mostly I wish to purchase some necessities that will be unavailable." He cleared his throat before looking intently at his plate and shoving a larger-than-acceptable piece of potato into his mouth.

"Well, I'm certain Nora would be happy to accompany you to any theater you wish to attend," her father offered.

Nora looked at him with wide eyes. What was he doing? He made it sound as if she was a horse the Admiral could take out for a turn.

She cleared her throat. "I'm certain, Papa, that the Admiral is not in want of company for the theater."

The Admiral swallowed hard. "I would not . . .be opposed to the idea." He whispered next to her. "But perhaps you would be more amiable to a walk? Perhaps tomorrow afternoon?"

Chapter Three

The words were out of his mouth before he even knew what he had said. A walk? Did he even wish to go for a turn with Miss Pemberton? He glanced at her from the corner of his eye. Well, he didn't *not* want to go for a walk with her.

He pushed his glasses up on his nose. He should concentrate on finding a wife who could go with him to New Zealand, not wasting time on a handsome lady who knew nothing of hardship or trials. He would surely not find what he was looking for in a wife among the aristocracy.

Jeremy offered a small smile to Miss Pemberton. It seemed they were to go on a walk tomorrow afternoon. It was not as if he could take the offer back now, not that he wanted to. Or did he? Lud. When had he become so indecisive? Besides, what would it hurt if they took a turn? Was he not in London to enjoy some of the pleasures he would miss once he left? Miss Pemberton was a pleasure, was she not?

Miss Pemberton ate very little of the food on her plate. She pushed the potatoes back and forth, giving the appearance that she had eaten far more than she really had. Had she not a healthy appetite, or was there something else preventing her from eating?

"What are you to do after completing your post in New Zealand?" Miss Pemberton didn't look at him as she continued to distribute her food about her plate.

"I'm hopeful the post will earn me a new ship." Jeremy finished the last of his dessert and leaned back in his chair, wiping his mouth with his napkin.

"Then you do not intend to retire?" Lady Pemberton asked.

"Lud, my dear. Jeremy is only nine and thirty. He's far too young to retire. Even if he must spend the next two years in a most primitive post." Lord Pemberton folded his napkin and placed it beside his plate. "I'd say he has at least another ten years to give the Navy."

"Ten years?" Lady Pemberton gasped. "By the time he returns to England to stay, he shall be an old man."

Lord Pemberton looked affronted. "My dear, I'm two and fifty. Are you suggesting you're now married to an old man?"

Lady Pemberton blushed. "Oh, dearest. I had not even considered the possibility." She smiled lovingly at her husband and patted his hand. "But then, you always have seemed younger than your days."

Lord Pemberton shook his head, but there was a gleam in his eyes. "And now she's accusing me of being juvenile." He winked, and Jeremy grinned at him.

Lady Pemberton let out a huff of impatience. "I said nothing of the sort."

Jeremy glanced over at Miss Pemberton. How did she react to her parents' playful banter? It would mortify many young ladies. But he was pleased to see her smiling fondly at both of her parents. Indeed, the look of utter joy on her face nearly took his breath away. It was so different from her normally reserved demeanor.

Who could have known that look lay just beneath the surface? The knowledge made Jeremy want to scratch a little deeper and perhaps see what else Miss Pemberton was hiding. He frowned. He didn't have time for such things.

~

JEREMY PUSHED through the door of his rented apartment. He sucked in a deep breath, relieved to be away from Lady Pemberton and her penetrating questions. *Do you plan to keep a wife on a ship for ten years? Would it not be best if you waited to marry until you returned? You would be content with a widow, would you not?* His head ached from all the questions.

His valet, Marlowe, met him at the door. "May I take your beaver and your greatcoat, sir?"

Jeremy shrugged out of his coat and handed everything over to Marlowe.

"I hope your evening was pleasant, sir."

"Most aspects were."

"Most?" Marlowe pushed. It would never have been allowed by most gentlemen, but Marlowe and Jeremy were not like most masters and valets.

"Lord Pemberton was just as diverting as always." Jeremy grinned at the memory. "However, his wife had many questions she wished answered, many of which I had no answer to give her."

"I've a brandy waiting for you in the library." Marlowe grinned as he moved to the rack hanging just inside the hallway.

"Thank you." Marlowe had been with Jeremy's family for almost as long as Jeremy could remember. He had taken it upon himself to act as butler and footman while they were in London. Not that the flat was big enough to need either, but Marlowe insisted that someone of Jeremy's rank should not be without proper servants, no matter the size of his accommodations. Although, if Marlowe had his way, Jeremy would reside in a townhouse that was much too big for a single man.

Jeremy moved toward the room functioning as both his library and study and, on some occasions, his parlor. He sank into the couch and lifted the glass of liquid to his lips as he kicked off his shoes. Stretching out his legs, he crossed his ankles and rested his feet on the low table in front of him. The recently stoked fire flamed, and he allowed the heat to penetrate his stockings and warm him from the toes upward.

"I'm happy that Lord Pemberton is well. Did he bring anyone besides his wife to London with him?" Marlowe asked as he picked up Jeremy's discarded shoes.

Jeremy unbuttoned his tailcoat. Shrugging out of it, he draped it over a chair. "Yes, two of his daughters."

"Two daughters?" Jeremy didn't miss the interest in his valet's voice.

"Yes. The oldest Miss Pemberton is recently married. Her younger sisters, Miss Hanora and Miss Elizabeth, accompanied their parents."

Marlowe scratched his chin and frowned. "And what did you think of the ladies?"

Jeremy took a long sip of his drink and rested the glass on the arm of the couch. "The younger one is too young. She can't be more than eighteen or nineteen."

"What of the older Miss Pemberton?"

Jeremy shrugged. "She may not fare well in the wilds of New Zealand. She's very reserved and rarely looks a person in the eye." Jeremy sighed. At his introduction to Miss Pemberton, he had seen little to intrigue him. And in their conversation before dinner, he'd hardly been able to hold her gaze. However, things had improved during dinner, but he was uncertain they had improved enough. "I think I shall have to look elsewhere to find a match."

Marlowe stared down at Jeremy. "It was one evening. You're not going to give her more of a chance than that?"

"If I didn't know better, I should think the Pembertons were a relation of yours, Marlowe. You seem awfully determined to see me attached to one of the Pemberton ladies." Jeremy shifted in his seat. "Besides, I need a wife who can adapt quickly. I'm afraid Miss Pemberton will require too much time to adjust."

Marlowe smirked down at him.

Jeremy motioned to the other end of the couch. "Do sit

down, Marlowe. I'll not have you standing over me as if you're my schoolmaster scolding me."

"It isn't the Pemberton ladies as much as I wish to see you married." Marlowe sat down and twisted so he was more fully facing Jeremy. "It was my understanding that Sir Thompson expects you to take a wife to New Zealand. I would hate to see you lose the opportunity simply because you could not find a suitable lady."

"And you believe Miss Hanora Pemberton to be a suitable lady?"

Marlowe shrugged. "Perhaps. How can you know for certain after only one evening together?"

Years at sea had left Jeremy with few close friends. And Marlowe had, over the years, become as much of a friend as a valet, which was why Jeremy allowed such intimacies with him. He was grateful to have someone with whom to talk things out.

"I've not discounted Miss Pemberton, but nor am I convinced of her suitability." He took a sip and stared at the flames in the grate. "I'm to take a turn with her tomorrow. Perhaps I'll discover more."

Marlowe grinned. "Perhaps she'll be up to the task. She convinced you to take a turn with her, did she not? And after you had found her unsuitable. I believe that should be a point in her favor."

Jeremy's head shook. "Don't give her the credit. She had nothing to do with it. The words simply blurted out of my mouth before I even considered them."

Marlowe's brow rose. "Then she deserves even more credit. You do nothing without fully analyzing it. If this lady had you so off-kilter that you did anything without first considering it, she may just be up to the task."

Jeremy rolled his eyes. "Cleverness is not the only trait I'm looking for. She must also have a calm nature and perseverance. It will not be an easy go of it in New Zealand. The last thing I need is a lady who will turn into a watering pot simply because she hasn't attended a ball or the theater in a month." Jeremy tugged at his earlobe. He caught his contradiction, and it surprised him Marlowe had not called him out. Had he not complained that she was too reserved? Now he complained that she was not reserved enough? Again with his indecision. What was wrong with him?

"And if Miss Pemberton does not prove to be the best choice, what shall you do then?" Marlowe settled into the cushions. "You don't have the luxury of time, sir. Are you certain they will not allow you to take the post if you don't have a wife?"

Jeremy ran his hand down his face, tugging at his chin. "Sir Thompson seemed rather insistent on that point. They feel a lady will show the natives that we are there for peaceful reasons. But perhaps if I explain to Sir Thompson—" He didn't feel confident. "Although, I can't imagine he'll look favorably upon my next assignment should he have to find a replacement with short notice."

Jeremy took another sip of his drink before placing the glass on the tray. "It is why I'm concerned, Marlowe. Why am I wasting time walking about a park when I should focus on finding a proper wife?"

Marlowe's expression was bland. "Sir, you'll have to do some walking if you're to discover if any lady is up for the task." He leaned forward. "But keep in mind that it isn't only for this post that you should be considering. This wife will be yours even after you return from New Zealand. If you should not find someone you get on well with, I believe you'll be quite miserable for a very long time."

Jeremy shook his head. "But how is such a thing to be done in such a short amount of time?"

Marlowe shrugged. "Men do it every season. And some without ever meeting the lady at all." He gave Jeremy a wry smile. "I believe you're up to the task, sir. Perhaps you should not dismiss Miss Pemberton so quickly. She may just surprise you and turn out to be exactly who you need."

Jeremy narrowed his gaze at Marlowe. "Are you certain she

isn't a long-lost relative? Or do you have something else to gain from the union?"

Marlowe grinned. "The only thing I have to gain is your happiness."

Jeremy snorted. "Yes, we both know that's your main concern." He pushed himself to his feet and put his hands at his back, stretching out his muscles. "You shall have your wish, at least for now. I'll take a turn with her tomorrow. It is too late to back out now."

Jeremy moved toward the door, ready for sleep to put this whole mess from his mind. At least for a few hours.

"Just promise me you'll give her a chance," Marlowe called as Jeremy reached the door.

Jeremy nodded his head and waved a hand. "You have my word, Marlowe."

Chapter Four

Nora paced back and forth in front of the fireplace, twisting at the tips of her fingers until the blood leached from them. Why had her father suggested she accompany the Admiral to the theater? That was, after all, what had spurred the Admiral to ask her for a walk. Although a turn was far less intimate and quicker than an evening at the theater.

But at least on a walk, they could talk, which was not something they could do at the theater. While they had not spoken at length about much, she had very much enjoyed their conversation about his future and his fondness for the sea. Perhaps they could continue that conversation today.

She turned on her heel and made another pass.

He had told her he would fetch her at two, which left only ten minutes until his arrival. She would simply use the time to come up with some topics to discuss, should the *fondness of the sea* conversation wane.

She shook out her aching fingers. If she was to continue this worrying, she would need to discover a different way to exercise it, lest she twist off all the skin from her fingertips.

Higgins stepped into the room and cleared his throat. "Miss

Pemberton, the Admiral has come and is waiting in the Ivory Salon."

Nora clasped her hands tightly behind her back. He was early. Did that mean he wished to get the walk over with quickly? Or did he wish to start the walk sooner? He was a military man. Perhaps it was simply his way.

She gave her head an angry shake. Why did she care? It was not as if she expected anything to happen between them beyond the walk. While she would welcome his attentions, it was only a matter of time before he discovered her secret and that would be the end of it. Would it not be better for her if she did not allow herself to need him?

"I shall be along directly." She took several steps toward the door. For a fleeting moment, Nora considered staying where she was. If there was no walk, there could be no disappointment. She was tired of disappointment.

However, her previous disappointments were not the Admiral's fault, and he should not have to pay the price.

Nora moved over to the large mirror hanging over the side table and straightened her wig ever so slightly, making certain her curls hung directly in front of her ears. She was becoming more accustomed to seeing it there.

Turning her head from one side to the other, she studied her reflection as if seeing herself for the first time. Did she like what she saw? Could she tell it was a wig?

Her shoulders slumped.

Indeed, she didn't like what she saw, and she could most certainly tell it was a wig. But perhaps that was only because she knew the truth. The problem with trying to see yourself for the first time was that it never really was the first time. She already knew too much to be objective. If only she had a trusted friend who could tell her the truth. She didn't believe a word her mother or sister said about it.

Taking in a deep breath, she squared her shoulders and stared hard into the mirror. She would just have to pretend to have confidence if for no other reason than to save her family from humiliation. For her, it was already too late.

Reluctantly, Nora left the privacy of the parlor to greet her guest properly.

She stepped through the salon doorway and stopped. The Admiral stood in front of a bookcase with his back to her. She stared, even though it was rude.

He cut a handsome form, even from behind. Broad shoulders tapered down to a trim waist. His hair curled up slightly at his collar. There were surely dozens of ladies in London who would welcome his attention. Why, then, was he standing in her salon?

She sighed. It was not him she didn't wish to be with, but rather people in general. The more she was out, the more likely she would be discovered.

"Admiral Fagan, it is a pleasure to see you again." Had she infused enough enthusiasm into her words?

The Admiral turned toward her, and his lips turned slightly upwards. Was it a genuine smile? He clasped his hands behind his back and took several steps toward her. "I can assure you, Miss Pemberton, that the pleasure is all mine."

Nora took several steps into the room, bringing them within a few yards of each other. She tilted her head and offered him a smile that she did not really feel. But as she looked at him and his slightly upturned lips, her smile increased. Perhaps she *did* mean it.

"You asked me to take a turn, sir." She glanced at the clock on the mantle. "But it is too early to be fashionable in Hyde Park."

Again, his lips turned up slightly, and Nora's copied.

"As you likely discovered last evening, I don't enjoy crowds."

They had something in common. Her chest warmed.

"I had thought we might explore a smaller park. Perhaps we could walk around St. James Square."

Nora's nose curled. "You wish to take a turn about St. James? But there isn't even grass. And the pond is surely still iced over. I don't believe there are even any ducks within. It is nothing compared to Hyde Park. Even Hanover or Berkeley Square would be preferable." She stared at him, wondering if it was crowds he didn't like or if he just did not wish to be seen with her. She pushed away the thought. If that was the case, why had he asked her?

He lifted his glasses off his nose and polished them with a cloth from his pocket. "It may not be as fine as others, but it is pretty enough. And I believe it will give us a chance to talk without all the interruptions that might come with other parks."

Nora nodded but she didn't know why. He was correct, they were likely to be some of the only people in St. James Square. They might encounter others using the square as a means of a shorter path to somewhere else, but few walked there for pleasure. The more she thought about it, the more amiable the plan became. "Very well. Shall we go?"

"Indeed, I've been looking forward to our outing all morning." Was he sincere? She didn't know him well enough to tell.

She stepped into the entryway, the Admiral just behind her, and Higgins stepped out of the cloakroom with her pelisse and bonnet.

Lizzie appeared on the landing above, hurrying down the stairs in a very unladylike fashion. "I'm sorry to keep you waiting, Nora. Mama insisted I change my dress before we left."

"I thought Penny was to accompany us."

Lizzie shook her head. "No, Mama felt it would be more appropriate for me to accompany you." She leaned in and put her hand to her lips. "I believe she is hoping I'll learn something more than just providing you with a chaperone. She believes I know nothing of how to act with a gentleman." Lizzie gave a disgusted snort.

Nora smiled. "At least you have the chance to leave the house. Mama has hardly let you out since we came to London."

"I suppose you're correct," Lizzie grinned. "Although I should not think I'll get a proper introduction to Hyde Park. We are leaving much too early to be there at the fashionable hour."

"We are not to walk about Hyde Park today. The Admiral wishes to take a turn around St. James Square."

"St. James?" The curl in Lizzie's nose left no doubt as to her opinions on the location. "But we walk there all the time. Why not simply take a turn about our own gardens?"

"Lower your voice, Lizzie." Nora glanced over her shoulder at the Admiral. She expected a scowl or at the very least a frown. But instead she found that same slight smile occupying his lips. Interesting. Perhaps he was not as dour as she had originally believed.

"We spend time in St. James often, but the Admiral hasn't had such an opportunity. If that's where he wishes to walk, we can certainly oblige him."

Nora turned toward him. "Shall we go?"

He nodded his head and lifted his arm. She placed her hand there and smiled up at him.

He looked down at her hand on his arm and frowned. Only then did Nora realize he had been motioning her toward the door.

Her face blazed. She jerked her hand away and clasped them firmly in front of her. How could she have been such a dolt?

The Admiral clasped his hands behind his back as if to inform her she was not welcome on his arm.

They stepped outside and Nora breathed in deeply. She didn't believe she had ever been happier to feel the crisp, cool air on her face.

Chapter Five

Why had he dropped his arm when she put her hand there? He had been motioning her toward the door, but he was not opposed to the contact. Even if it had heated his skin through his coats and sent tingles up his arm. That was still no reason to have reacted the way he did.

But he had not ended it there. No, he had added insult to injury by clasping his hands behind his back.

He pushed his glasses back up onto the bridge of his nose as they stepped out onto the walkway. His thumb rubbed lightly over the back of his hand where tingles still danced across his skin.

If he offered her his arm now, what would she do? Lud, he had made a muddle of this. But why? It was not as if he had never had a lady on his arm. His time at sea left him less confident with ladies than other gentlemen of his acquaintance. But confidence was not his problem. Or was it?

He sighed, and she glanced up at him. He smiled down at her, trying to lessen the tension hanging between them.

They passed over the roadway and made their way to the small pond. An iron fence separated them from the water and the statue of William III.

Miss Pemberton focused on the homes in front of her as she

walked. "How long are you to be stationed in New Zealand?" she asked in a tight voice.

Was she back to not looking at him?

"The post is of an undetermined time. It will depend on several factors. If I can forge a relationship with the natives, then I expect it shall be for at least two years. However, if they do not accept me, my stay may be very short-lived."

"It sounds as if it could be dangerous."

He glanced over at her and then looked off into the distance. Did she fear for him? That thought brought warmth to his chest. "I suppose there is an element of danger. Those who went before me rarely made a good impression. But I hope to change that." He looked over at her again, but this time didn't look away. "Have you ever thought of leaving England?"

"Sometimes." She looked down. "More so recently. Although, I suspect my imaginings are nothing like reality." Miss Pemberton held his gaze.

He sucked in a breath and smiled down at her. Lud, she was a handsome woman.

"Two years is a long time to be away from England."

"And that's only this assignment. Until I retire, I'll be gone more than not." He shrugged. "But I've been away from England for most of my life. I know nothing else."

They continued walking beside the wrought-iron fence and started their second time around. A silence fell over them, but it was not an uncomfortable one—which he found unexpected.

As they started their third turn about the pond, Jeremy looked to his right. "I imagine it is the gardens behind many of these houses that contain the real beauty."

Miss Pemberton nodded and followed his gaze. "That house belongs to Lord Derby. While I've never seen them, I have heard his gardens are some of the finest in London."

"It is too bad we can't take a turn about them. I'm certain they would delight every bit as much as Hyde Park but without all the people."

She tilted her head and peered around him. "Perhaps we could apply to the housekeeper?"

Miss Elizabeth stepped up beside them. "If we were to walk down that alleyway, we would find ourselves in Lord Derby's gardens. There is no reason to apply to the housekeeper."

"No, Lizzie." Miss Pemberton held out her hand, but Miss Elizabeth pulled away.

"Then stay here if you wish." She bounded off.

Jeremy opened his mouth, then shut it. He looked at the house and then back to Miss Pemberton. "That is most improper. One does not impose on another's gardens without an invitation."

"I'm well aware of such facts, sir." She glanced at her sister's back. "Lord Derby is certainly away at Lords. We will not stay long—but I cannot leave Lizzie here alone." The cold air created a cloud in front of Miss Pemberton's mouth.

"You can't be serious." Jeremy stopped walking and stared at her. "What would you do if you found someone walking your gardens?"

Miss Pemberton shrugged. "I suppose it would depend upon who it was. If it were an upstanding member of the Royal Navy and the daughters of a baron, innocently taking a turn in a lovely garden, I should have no qualms about it. Besides, we will be so quick, no one will ever know."

His head shook but then stopped as he looked at her imploring face.

"I have to go after her, Admiral."

"It is a great risk." He looked around.

"It is. But I'll take risks for those I love." Miss Pemberton lifted her chin. "I had thought, Admiral, you might have a bit more backbone about you."

Jeremy stared at her. Such loyalty was not easily found, even for a loved one. He narrowed his eyes for a moment then nodded. "Very well. But only if you promise to make haste."

She ducked her head. "Thank you, sir."

Jeremy put out his hand, bringing her to a stop. "I'll have you know I am not a coward."

She bit her lip again, but he thought it might be to keep from laughing. Was she laughing at him? It should make him angry, but he found the opposite true. His lips quirked up, as did a brow.

"My apologies, sir." She looked down at his hand, and he regretfully dropped it away. "I was not inferring you are a coward—that you lacked an adventurous nature, perhaps, but certainly not a coward." Did he detect a note of sauciness in her voice?

His mouth dropped open slightly as they walked quickly in the direction Miss Elizabeth had gone. "You believe me devoid of an adventurous nature? Does not fighting Napoleon on the high seas count as adventurous?"

"Perhaps," Miss Pemberton gave an exaggerated shrug. "But is it not your duty? When it becomes your occupation, it loses some of its adventure, does it not?" This time, she could not hold back the smile.

They crossed over the road to the walkway in front of Lord Derby's house. Jeremy folded his arms across his chest. He could not believe they were about to do this. "Where did Miss Elizabeth go?"

"There is a small alleyway that leads to the mews. If we follow that, there should be an entrance to the garden just before."

He held out his arm. "Please, lead the way."

They strolled down the alley until they came to a gate. If they had not been looking for it, they likely would've walked right past it as vines and shrubbery made it nearly invisible.

Nora looked over her shoulder and raised her brows. "Here it is, the entrance to Lord Derby's gardens."

Jeremy straightened his coat and squared his shoulders. If he was to do it, he planned to do it with confidence, as if he had every reason to be in Lord Derby's garden. He only hoped Sir Thompson did not hear of it.

He lifted his arm, and Nora stared down at it. Lud, would she not take it? He had already embarrassed her once with this situation.

Jeremy stared at her. "If we are to be caught, I should prefer we look as if we belong. A lie can go a long way if you look as though it is the truth."

Miss Pemberton's brow wrinkled. "You're proficient at lying then, sir?"

He shook his head. "Certainly not. But I've done my share of spying. The principles are similar, even if the motives are different."

A grin curved Miss Pemberton's lips and she tilted her head. "I find I enjoy thinking of Lord Derby as the enemy." She lifted her hand and placed it on his arm. "Now, sir, what's our next move for spying on the enemy?"

"Simple," he released his breath. "Act as though we are doing nothing untoward."

They pushed through the gate but paused when Miss Elizabeth was not in view on the other side.

"Where is she?" Jeremy looked from side to side.

"She must have gone farther in."

"Of course she did," Jeremy grunted.

They closed the gate and stepped through the arch in the hedgerow. Miss Pemberton stopped and pulled Jeremy back as a small breath sucked through her slightly parted lips. "Gracious. It is beautiful."

Jeremy looked over at her and smiled. "I didn't know something could be so beautiful in the winter."

Miss Elizabeth stood in front of a tree just ahead.

"Lizzie," Miss Pemberton hissed. "It isn't proper for you to be strolling around the garden without an invitation."

"I'm only taking a peek," Miss Elizabeth whined.

Miss Pemberton stomped her foot. "If they catch us, I shall tell Papa it was all your fault."

Miss Elizabeth nodded. "We won't be caught."

Patches of color dotted the garden, but the predominant

colors were white and varying shades of green against the thin layer of snow still clinging to the ground.

Jeremy released a breath. "We've had a peek. We should leave before someone sees us." He turned toward the gate.

Miss Pemberton reached out and grabbed his arm. "Do you not wish to see more?" Her voice came out quiet—almost reverent.

He narrowed his eyes and shook his head. "We were not going to stay."

"We shall not stay for long." Miss Pemberton pulled him deeper into the garden. What had happened to her resistance?

She stopped in front of a bush. Few leaves still hung from the branches, but several pink and white blossoms remained. Miss Pemberton leaned toward a bunch still in their prime. She breathed in deeply and hummed. "Do you not love the smell of honeysuckle?"

Jeremy shrugged. "I don't know that I've ever smelled it before."

She moved to the side and motioned him forward. "Then it is good we didn't leave. Otherwise, you would still not have had the pleasure."

Jeremy held her gaze for a moment before leaning forward and sniffing the flowers. "It would seem I told you an untruth just now, Miss Pemberton."

Nora raised her brows. "Oh?"

"I have smelled this flower before. I simply didn't know the name. My mother used to wear this scent when I was a boy." He leaned forward, taking in another breath and closing his eyes. He had not thought about his mother in weeks. Perhaps even months. A knot formed in his stomach. How could that be? He vowed to write to his brother this very evening and instruct him to have honeysuckle planted at Wayside Lodge.

Miss Pemberton moved farther down the pebbled path. Large clumps of pink flowers broke through the crusty snow, interspersed with the white and green patches dotting the ground. "What are those?" He pointed to the white flowers.

"Those are Christmas Roses." She dropped to her knees. "And these are pink Daphne."

Jeremy dropped down to his haunches beside her. "Do you know the names of all the flowers?" He reached forward and lightly clasped one of the pink flowers.

"Most of them."

He looked over at her. "How do you know them?"

"We have many of the same flowers in our winter garden." She ducked her head slightly. "I'm rather fond of flowers, so our gardener always asks for my preferences."

Jeremy shook his head slowly. "If we could have seen the same thing in your gardens, why did we not just take a turn there?"

Miss Elizabeth stepped up beside them. "You did not ask to see our gardens. You asked to walk in St. James Square."

Jeremy smirked at her. "I didn't know it was an option." He turned his gaze back to Miss Pemberton. Lifting a hand, he pushed one of her curls back away from her cheek.

Her eyes widened, and she drew away from him. He frowned. What had he been thinking to act in such an untoward way?

"I beg your pardon. What are you doing in our garden?" A voice shrieked from the distance.

Both Jeremy and Miss Pemberton jumped quickly to their feet.

An older woman stared at them with her hands on her hips.

"I—I beg your pardon. We—we—that is to say—" Jeremy stammered. Had not both Pemberton ladies promised they would not be caught?

Miss Pemberton put her hand on his arm and gave it a gentle squeeze. She took a step forward. "Excuse us, Lady Derby. This is my fault. My mother, Lady Pemberton, told me just last night how lovely your gardens were. The Admiral and I were walking around the pond in the square, and I mentioned your gardens to him."

Jeremy looked over at her sincere face and a chuckle bubbled up. He coughed and covered his lips with his hand. It seemed he wasn't the only one who could tell a bouncer.

"I told him we would only peek and that you wouldn't mind. My mother mentioned you offered for her to take a turn about them."

Lady Derby's brow furrowed and Jeremy grunt-laughed. He should not be finding humor in this situation, but he could not seem to help himself.

"The invitation was extended . . . *for spring*." The lady enunciated her words. "Not while it is still winter."

Miss Pemberton straightened her shoulders and back. "I had supposed that to be the case. I only wished to peek." She put her hand to her chest. "But when I saw how exquisite your garden was, even in the winter, I could not help but come in farther." She motioned back to Jeremy. "And I dragged the poor Admiral and my sister along, I'm afraid."

Jeremy crinkled his brow, hoping he looked adequately displeased with the situation.

"Winter gardens rarely warrant praise—they are usually rather lackluster." Miss Pemberton stepped forward and dipped down to the nearby pink Daphne. "But your gardens are truly lovely, even in the winter. How could one not stay and enjoy the beauty?"

Lady Derby's frown melted into a smile. "The gardens are nothing compared to what they will look like in the spring and summer. But I confess, I have spent many hours overseeing their plantings and ensuring there is color even in the winter." She moved next to Miss Pemberton. "Tell me, Miss Pemberton, which is your favorite flower?"

Miss Pemberton glanced over her shoulder at Jeremy and winked before turning her attention to Lady Derby. "While the pink Daphne is lovely, I think my favorite is the purple Heather."

Jeremy stared at her as the two ladies chatted amiably for several minutes. He would never have guessed this vivacious woman lived inside Miss Pemberton.

Lady Derby sighed contentedly and turned her gaze to Jeremy. "And what do you think of my little garden, sir?"

"I've seen nothing of its equal, my lady." Jeremy gazed at Miss Pemberton. Did she realize he was not only speaking of the garden?

Pulling her dress to the side, Miss Pemberton curtsied. "Please accept my apologies, my lady. We should never have presumed to invade your sanctuary." She reached out and tugged on Jeremy's arm. "Thank you for your hospitality. We will leave you to your garden. Good day, my lady."

As they reached the gate, Lady Derby called back to them. "Please, come back in the springtime."

Miss Pemberton paused long enough to offer a small wave. "You could not keep me away."

They all hurried through the gate and into the small alleyway leading to the mews.

"I hope you're satisfied, Lizzie. I'm certain mama and papa will hear of this even if I don't say a word." Miss Pemberton stood with her hands on her hips.

Miss Elizabeth shrugged. "It turned out for the best."

Miss Pemberton's eyes widened but no words escaped her lips.

"Indeed, it turned out well, thanks to Miss Pemberton's quick thinking." He grinned, hoping she would not be angry.

"Admiral Fagan, please accept my apol—"

He held up his hand. "You need not apologize, Miss Pemberton. As I said, everything turned out for the best." He was surprised to realize he meant what he said. He had seen a lovely garden that reminded him of his mother. And he had learned a great deal about Miss Pemberton. How could he regret the events? He was uncertain where his knew information would lead, but Marlowe would surely have some opinions.

Chapter Six

"Are you ready to admit yet that I was right?" Marlowe placed a tray on the low table.

"And just what were you right about?" Jeremy had an idea, but he did not wish to give Marlowe the win.

"You enjoyed your walk with Miss Pemberton. I saw it on your face when you returned." He leaned forward with raised brows. "You were smiling."

Jeremy narrowed his eyes. "That's absurd."

"Yes, I found it rather unbelievable as well. Rear Admiral Fagan rarely smiles."

Jeremy scoffed. "That's not what I was speaking of. The notion that you could see it on my face is what's absurd."

"Very well. I'll stop with the absurdities." He poured some brandy into a glass on the tray and handed it over to Jeremy. "Your brandy, sir."

Jeremy took the glass and sipped the liquid slowly before setting it on the arm of the couch. "That is not to say I didn't enjoy myself. Miss Pemberton is quite different from what I thought her to be."

Marlowe nodded, but Jeremy could see the smile his valet was trying to suppress. "How is that, sir?"

Jeremy sighed. What had he expected of her? He had thought her to be reserved, which for most of their time together she had been. But once she entered the garden, it was as if a whole new person emerged. The question plaguing him now was which person was her usual form?

"She was different. Her eyes shone with excitement and perhaps . . . wonderment? And the lady is quite adept at telling a bouncer when the need arises."

Marlowe folded his arms across his chest, but Jeremy shook his head and motioned him onto the end of the sofa. "You should have seen her when Lady Derby caught us in her gardens. By the time we left, the lady was inviting us back again."

Marlowe's brow furrowed. "You were caught in Lady Derby's gardens? Her private gardens?"

Jeremy nodded absently. "Yes, Miss Elizabeth wished to see them and ran inside before we could stop her. We had to retrieve her. Miss Pemberton would not abide leaving the girl to face punishment alone if she were caught." He swallowed another sip from his glass. "Miss Pemberton is fiercely loyal to those she loves. It is a fine quality; do you not agree?"

Marlowe stared, speechless.

"You do not agree, Marlowe?"

The valet shook his head. "Pardon me, sir. I didn't hear what you said after the part where you entered a private garden without permission." He leaned forward and narrowed his gaze. "Are you feeling unwell, sir?"

Jeremy smirked at him. "I am well, Marlowe. And it isn't as if it was my idea. I was simply there to aid Miss Pemberton in fetching her sister." He shrugged. "Once inside though, she was a different person. Her gaze lifted and she spoke to me, not the ground. And her knowledge of the plants was quite vast. I can hardly account for the change."

"Perhaps it was the garden, sir. Perhaps there she felt secure to show more of her true nature."

Jeremy frowned. "Then you think that's the true Miss Pemberton?"

"It seems likely. Is that undesirable?"

"I don't know." Jeremy rubbed at his chin. "She was very diplomatic with Lady Derby, which could prove useful. And she did display an adeptness for lying, which has its advantages and disadvantages." He shook his head. "But it is doubtful there will be many winter gardens in New Zealand. If that's the only place she is comfortable, she'll be of little help to me."

Marlowe's head shook. "It's not the garden itself, sir, but rather what it represents."

"The garden represented something?" Jeremy looked skeptically across the couch.

"Yes. In the garden she's knowledgeable. It is a place where she likely feels safe acting in a way society might not accept. There is peace in that." He crossed his arms again. "You would simply need to find a replacement for the garden."

"What kind of replacement?"

Marlowe shrugged. "That's what you must discover." He grinned. "Perhaps more walks are in order."

Jeremy downed the rest of his brandy. "Hmmm." He grunted. "Discover what can replace the garden. How the devil am I to do that?"

Marlowe stood up and took the glass from Jeremy's hand. "You'll know when you find it, sir."

Jeremy ran a hand through his hair and down the back of his neck. "Sometimes I think you only complicate matters for me."

The valet grinned. "I'm pleased to be of service, sir."

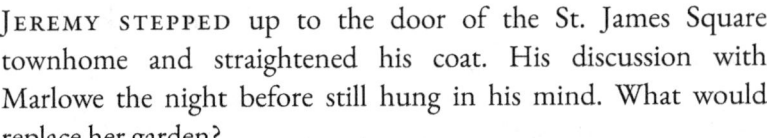

JEREMY STEPPED up to the door of the St. James Square townhome and straightened his coat. His discussion with Marlowe the night before still hung in his mind. What would replace her garden?

He sighed. Did he even want to find a replacement? It seemed like long, tedious work that he had not the time nor inclination to pursue. Perhaps he should look elsewhere for a wife.

He glanced up at the white stone facade. Did he wish to look someplace else? It made sense in his head to search elsewhere, but he couldn't bring himself to do it. His inclination was to see Miss Pemberton again.

She reminded him of an onion. Every time he peeled away a layer, there was another one beneath that was more interesting than the last. Just how many layers she had, he didn't know. But perhaps that was why he was standing there.

There had been one part of his walk with Miss Pemberton that he had not shared with Marlowe. When he had pushed the curl away from her cheek, he had very nearly kissed her. Luckily, Lady Derby had discovered them.

He released his breath and knocked on the door. Wool-gathering was not helping him in the least.

The butler answered and dipped his head to Jeremy. "Good day, sir."

Jeremy produced a card and handed it over. "Good day. Is Miss Pemberton at home?"

The butler motioned Jeremy inside and led him down a corridor. "Please wait here, sir." The butler left Jeremy alone in the parlor.

Did Jeremy even like onions? He shrugged. They *did* enhance a meal that might otherwise be dull. That certainly seemed to describe Miss Pemberton. He thought for a moment. Yes, he could say with a surety that he liked onions.

"Lady Pemberton informed me that Miss Pemberton is in the garden. If you would follow me, I shall take you to her."

Jeremy nodded.

She was in the garden. Marlowe's words came back to him. *That is where she likely finds peace.* Jeremy nodded. Of course. Why had he not seen it sooner? The garden was to Miss Pemberton as the sea was to Jeremy. That's what Marlowe had meant, was it not? Jeremy simply needed to discover what it was about the garden that made her feel comfortable and then give that to her in a different way. But how was he to do that? It seemed Marlowe was correct again. Jeremy needed to spend more time with Miss Pemberton. He grinned. That was not such a terrible prospect.

The butler pushed through the terrace doors and led Jeremy over the grass to a hedgerow. He motioned to a narrow gap. "She's in there, sir."

Jeremy paused before entering the garden. Would she be happy to see him? Had she thought about him as much as he had thought about her? He didn't know how that could be possible.

Pushing himself forward, he stepped through the hedge and came up short. Miss Pemberton sat on the ground, a spade in one hand and her fingers digging into what was surely frigid dirt. A quiet, lovely tune drifted on the breeze.

Jeremy stood rooted in place. Lud, she was prettier than he remembered, if that was possible. He cleared his throat and the humming stopped. Regret washed over him.

She turned and looked up at him in surprise. "Admiral Fagan."

Jeremy's smile grew as he noticed a streak of dirt running the length of her cheekbone. "I'm sorry to intrude. I can return later if you wish." He knew he was staring, but he could not help himself.

"No. Please, stay." Miss Pemberton stood up, but she didn't hold his gaze.

She was in her garden. Why was she not acting as she had in Lord Derby's garden? Jeremy frowned. Marlowe was bacon-brained. Or Jeremy was for listening to the valet.

She shook the dirt from her apron. "How nice of you to visit." Her tone didn't sound as if she thought it was nice. It was strained and tight.

She clapped her hands together and dust blew into the air. "I'm sorry you had to see me like this." She pressed the back of her hand to her temple and her eyes widened slightly. She glanced quickly over at him and then dropped her gaze. "If you'll give me a moment, I shall hurry inside and wash my hands."

"Please, don't. I do not mind if you wish to continue what you were doing."

She slowly raised her eyes to meet his. "If you're certain, I'll finish the last bit of seeds."

"This is the famous winter garden we should have walked in yesterday?" He looked around. While he hated to belittle anything of Miss Pemberton's, this garden was nothing to Lady Derby's.

"No, actually. This is the kitchen garden." She kept her gaze on the dirt.

"Oh. I simply assumed." He bounced on the balls of his feet. "What are you planting?"

"Some carrots, lettuce, and herbs."

"I had thought perhaps Lady Derby's garden inspired you."

She looked over at him and her eyes lit. "How could one not find inspiration there?" She covered the seeds with fresh dirt and sat back on her heels. "Do you garden, Admiral?"

Jeremy moved closer, shaking his head. "As I've spent most of my life at sea, I have little experience with seeds and soil."

"That's a pity. It is one of my favorite things to do." Her hands moved back and forth, creating rows in the soil.

"It's not that I refuse to try." He shifted on his feet. "Indeed, once I arrive in New Zealand, I might try my hand at it."

Miss Pemberton closed her eyes and sucked in a breath. She patted the ground next to her. "Come, I'll give you a lesson." When she looked up at him, he could see the uncertainty in her gaze. "Although you probably do not wish to do so now. You're not dressed for gardening."

"Nonsense. I'm always eager to learn new skills." He dropped down to his haunches and pulled off his gloves. Plunging his hands into the soil, his little finger brushed against hers. Every instinct told him to pull away, but he fought them, leaving his hand beside hers. He looked at her from the corner of his eye to see if she minded and was relieved to see her smile.

"Now is a perfect time to try my hand. Would it not be a shame for me to arrive in New Zealand and have no experience at all?"

"Indeed, it would. Shall I fetch you an apron? I should not like to see you soil your good coat."

He shook his head. "Marlowe does not frighten me." He winked at her and then froze. What had he done? What was it about her that made him laugh at improper times or wink in the garden?

Miss Pemberton chuckled quietly. "Very well." She reached over and picked up his right hand. Turning it over, she rolled his fingers up slightly, forming a cup. Reaching for a small, folded paper, she pinched something between her fingers. Dropping them in the palm of his hand, Jeremy saw the smallest seeds he'd ever seen.

"What are these?" He moved his hand, allowing the seeds to fall one way and then the other, separating into small piles.

"They are carrot seeds. Have you never seen them before?" She dropped the seeds into the rows one at a time. Then gently pushed the soil over them.

"Is it not too cold?"

She shook her head. "No, this is the best time to plant carrots, when the soil is just soft enough to work but the air is still chilled. We don't want the seeds to freeze, but if we plant them now, we shall have a good harvest for summer and autumn."

Jeremy ran his hand through the soil. One by one, he dropped the seeds from his hand and then covered them over as he had watched her do.

"Nicely done, Admiral." She sat back on her heels and dusted off her hands.

Jeremy did the same. Then he stood up and offered her his hand.

She looked at it and bit her lip before taking hold and allowing him to help her up.

He extended his arm to her, wondering if she would take it. She placed her hand on his arm, barely touching the fabric of his coat.

He looked around the garden. "Did you plant all of this?"

Miss Pemberton's eyes traveled the same path as his. "No. Walters will plant the other seeds in another month or so. But he knows carrots and lettuce are my favorites, so he saves them for me."

"That is kind of him. You enjoy gardening, then?" Gads, what a mutton-brained thing to say. All evidence pointed to that notion. And had she not already mentioned it?

Merriment danced in her eyes. "Yes, I do—very much."

"Just vegetables?"

Gads. She was acting more as she had in Lady Derby's garden. It was *him* that had changed into a complete nodcock.

"I enjoy all kinds of gardening, although vegetables and herbs were not my favorite when I was young. But now I appreciate that they have a purpose beyond just beauty." Her face darkened, but it quickly disappeared.

"What else do you enjoy doing?" Jeremy reached up and tucked her hand into the crook of his arm, feeling more pleased with his situation than he had since leaving the ship.

The action had the opposite effect on Miss Pemberton. "My hands are too dirty." She kept her gaze on the ground in front of them, the ease of moments ago gone.

"Nonsense." He patted her hand.

She crinkled her brow. "I enjoy doing many things."

"Such as?" Jeremy looked up, only then noticing the footman standing at the terrace doors. They were not completely alone, which he supposed was advisable, even if disappointing. "I heard you singing when I came into the garden. It was lovely."

"Thank you. I enjoy singing for my family and close friends, but I'm more comfortable on the pianoforte. Even still, I don't enjoy performing." She licked her lips. "Mama says I must get over it. She says I play well enough to perform at any musicale." Her hand lifted to the curl at the side of her face and then dropped slowly down to her side. "But it is something I don't wish to do."

"I understand the feeling." Jeremy reached over and plucked a dried leaf from the tree, crumbling it between his fingers as they walked. "I'm content to watch the other performers."

Miss Pemberton's eyes lit. "You sing?"

Jeremy chuckled. "Nothing as lovely as you. But I sing a little for friends."

Miss Pemberton smiled. "Then perhaps while you're in London, we shall become friends and you will allow me to hear you sing." Her face pinked.

Jeremy straightened as warmth spread throughout his limbs. He had thought she was lovely before, but the heightened color only added to her beauty. His step faltered, but he quickly regained his composure.

He cleared his throat. "I should like that very much. But only if you promise to play while I sing."

She looked at the ground in front of her but nodded. "I should be delighted."

Jeremy looked over at her and studied her profile. Was she someone he could marry? Was she someone who could survive and even thrive in a place like New Zealand? Women capable of such a task were rare. But the more he came to know her, the more he believed she just might be the onion he was looking for.

Chapter Seven

Nora stepped inside the entryway of Lord Barnsby's London townhome just behind her parents. Crowds of people milled about, streaming in and out of the ballroom.

Nora took a step back from her parents and lifted a shaky hand to her hair. She patted at the wig even though she knew Penny had pinned everything in place. If she wished to keep her secret, she must quit touching it.

She was certain Admiral Fagan had noticed the movement of the wig when they were in the garden yesterday. But he had said nothing. He was too much of a gentleman.

This was it. This was where everything would come out...*if* she was not careful. Her mother had promised nothing would go amiss, but surely there were people there who could discern a wig from real hair. The only question was when they discovered her, would they reveal it to everyone present or keep it to themselves?

She recognized no one, which seemed to her advantage. It would be far easier for her to disappear among the crowds if no one were looking for her.

"Come along, Nora." Her mother reached for her arm,

guiding her toward the receiving line at the far end of the entry-way. "Let me introduce you to Lord and Lady Barnsby."

Nora clasped her hands in front of her to hide the tremor in her fingers. For at least the millionth time, she wished she'd had her Season last year. She was a nervous wreck, flinching at every chuckle or laugh—waiting for someone to expose her. She kept her gaze on the floor, only looking up when introductions were made.

Lady Barnsby was kind, and it allowed Nora to hope that others would be the same. Perhaps she might actually make it through this Season.

"Miss Pemberton," a voice sounded to her side. *Or perhaps she wouldn't.* Mr. Perry lifted a hand.

Nora glanced over at him before moving in behind her mother. But it was too late. He had seen her and was not to be deterred. He hurried across the entryway. "I had heard you were in London for the Season."

Nora looked up long enough to smile fleetingly. "Yes. My sister, Elizabeth, is also here, though she's not out in society yet." Gads, why was she rattling on? Surely he would move on if she remained quiet.

He smiled at her. "I hope you'll save the third set for me."

Nora nodded, even as she wished she could flee. "Of course." Large urns of pink and purple flowers filled alcoves and stood on pedestals in the corners, filling the ballroom with a sweet fragrance.

Just last year, Nora would have thrived in this environment. She had always loved the beauty of flowers and the thrill of a ball. But that was the old Nora.

Her mother tugged her over to a cluster of seating near the dance floor. Nora pulled away, instead heading for the grouping in the far back corner.

Her mother raised a brow but acquiesced.

"I shall retire to the card room, Charlotte. If you need me, you know where to find me." Her father pressed a kiss on her mother's cheek.

Her mother smiled and patted Nora's hand, looking up at her father. "Nothing shall go awry, Robert. Nora and I shall do very well on our own." Her mother's gaze drifted down the wall. "You see, there is Mrs. Hattersley. Come, Nora. Let's say hello."

Her father winked at them as he turned to leave.

"You go along, Mama. I'm content to stay here and watch the dancing." Nora sat down and released a sigh. Now it was a waiting game—waiting for the evening to end.

As if she had spoken her thoughts aloud, a man weaved his way through the group and stopped in front of her. He bowed deeply, looking up at her through his lashes. "Miss Pemberton, I hoped you would do me the honor of dancing the next set with me."

Would the fates never smile down on her? "Mr. Blakemore?" She hardly recognized him as the boy she had known. Her stomach clenched. He had always been rather observant. And critical. Although that had been before his father's factory had failed and the family had had to leave Derbyshire. Perhaps he had lost his critical nature.

Mr. Blakemore looked at her appraisingly.

Or perhaps he had not. Nora dropped her gaze to the floor, forcing herself not to lift a hand to her wig. If someone was to discover her, it would be Mr. Blakemore.

"Mr. Blakemore. It has been a long time. I hardly recognized you."

He stood before her, his stance rigid. "I don't blame you, Miss Pemberton. Unlike you, I've changed much since my days in Derbyshire." He lifted his arm for her to take. "Would you do me the honor of dancing the next set with me?"

Nora licked her lips. If she said no, she would ruin her chances of dancing for the rest of the evening—which didn't seem like such a punishment. But mama would surely ring a peal over her for it.

She nodded. "Indeed, thank you."

Mr. Blakemore led her to the dance floor and deposited her in the line, taking the spot directly across from her. She kept her eyes on the toes of her slippers.

Like most dances, she only had small moments when she must speak with him before she moved to a different partner. But in those few moments, he managed to tell her a great deal about himself. He had bought a commission in the Army and had only just sold it when his great-uncle died, leaving Mr. Blakemore to inherit. "The house isn't as grand as Blenheim or Chatsworth, but I believe you would find it a great deal nicer than Hollydale Hall." The old Nora would never have allowed anyone to insult her home. But she had not the luxury of drawing attention to herself with a scene.

The set lasted far longer than Nora would have liked. At every turn, she half expected her wig to slip from her head. When she was not worrying over that, she was forced to listen to Mr. Blakemore criticize everything around them.

When at last he led her back to her seat, her mother had finished her conversation with Mrs. Hattersley and now sat waiting for her. "Thank you for the set, Miss Pemberton." He looked at her mother. "Lady Pemberton." He bowed, then turned and disappeared into the crowd.

Her mother's fan fluttered furiously. "He cuts a fine form." She sighed. "It is too bad his family comes from manufacturing."

"You have not heard? He has inherited an estate in Devonshire from his great-uncle." Nora looked over at her mother. "He's certain I would find the house even lovelier than Hollydale Hall."

Her mother raised her chin and huffed. "I had thought to invite him to dinner."

"I'm glad you didn't. I don't think either of us could endure such an evening." Nora glanced around the room discreetly. She could only imagine the whispered comments being said about her. She pushed herself back against the seat, hoping to blend into the furniture.

If only the Admiral were in attendance. He would surely prove diverting. Although, even if he were in attendance, he would likely not single her out now that he knew about her wig.

"Miss Pemberton, I'm happy to see you here this evening." Her lips lifted even before her gaze. As if her wish had been granted, the Admiral stood before her, a slight smile on his lips. She was growing to adore that slight smile.

Her heart pounded in her ears. "Admiral Fagan, what a surprise. I didn't know you were to attend this ball."

The Admiral motioned to the chair next to her, and she nodded.

He sat and pulled down on his waistcoat. "I hope it isn't too unpleasant of a surprise."

"On the contrary. I'm very pleased to see you." She lifted a hand to her temple and glanced at him. He already knew about her wig. She need not be as careful around him. Or did she? Would he be there now if he knew?

"Miss Pemberton, I believe you promised me this set." Mr. Perry stood before her.

Nora nearly sighed. Why had Mr. Perry come just now? Why could he not have saved her from Mr. Blakemore? The Admiral would surely leave before she returned. And then who would Nora have to speak with?

Reluctantly, she stood and allowed Mr. Perry to lead her out onto the floor. They took their places, but Nora kept her gaze trained on Admiral Fagan. He still sat one seat away from her mother. Did that mean he was staying? Her lips twitched up.

The set dragged on nearly as long as it had with Mr. Blakemore, except this time it was not as much the conversation as it was the wrong partner. Not that Mr. Perry was objectionable, he was just not Admiral Fagan. Jeremy. Her face heated at the thought of his Christian name.

At last, Mr. Perry led her back to her seat. Jeremy—she held back a sigh—still sat where she had left him. Mr. Perry bowed. "Thank you for the dance, Miss Pemberton."

Nora looked at her toes. "Thank you, Mr. Perry. You're a fine dancer."

The Admiral cleared his throat and stood up, holding his hand out to her. "Is your next set taken, Miss Pemberton?"

Nora looked up at him, a flutter tumbling around in her stomach. "No one has claimed it, sir."

He helped her to her feet, then tucked her hand in the crook of his arm, just as he had when they'd been in the garden.

The first dance was a waltz, allowing her more time with the Admiral than she had had with Mr. Blakemore. Perhaps the fates were smiling on her at last.

The Admiral spoke less than either of her other partners, but she was far more comfortable and relaxed with him. Whenever he caught her gaze, he would smile, which made her smile. Gads, she must look like an idiot.

When the Admiral escorted Nora back to her mother, she expected him to make his excuses and remove to the card room or at least ask another young lady to dance. But to her surprise, he dropped into the seat next to her. She didn't know what to make of it. What would others think of it? They would surely take it as a sign of partiality. She looked at him from the corner of her eyes. The thought did not bother her.

She didn't miss Mr. Blakemore's raised brow from across the room.

The Admiral leaned over. "Miss Pemberton," he whispered in her ear. Gooseflesh rippled over her skin. "I wondered if you might accompany me on a carriage ride through Hyde Park tomorrow afternoon?"

Nora twisted in her seat, somewhat taken aback. Did he not despise Hyde Park? And yet, he asked her to accompany him there tomorrow?

She felt like squealing but settled for a smile. "I should be delighted, Admiral."

He unfolded his arms and stood up. "I suppose I shall see what's happening in the cardroom." He pulled at his waistcoat. "But first, may I claim your supper dance, Miss Pemberton."

Nora swallowed, uncertain what it all meant. "It isn't taken, sir."

The Admiral grinned and dipped his head to her. "Capital."

How had she once thought him dour?

He dipped his head to her mother then moved into the crowd, taking her ease with him.

Chapter Eight

Jeremy pulled a sleek, black chaise to a stop in front of the Pemberton townhouse.

A small tiger jumped from the step at the back and hurried to grab the reins. He scratched the nose of the horse, whispering calmly into its ear.

Jeremy stepped to the door and knocked firmly. He sucked in a breath as he straightened his waistcoat and then his tailcoat. Looking down, he frowned at the dust on his Hessians. *That will not do.*

Withdrawing a handkerchief from his pocket, he rubbed it across the toes of his boots. Straightening, he grimaced. He would never allow such shabby work from one of his officers.

He looked up and down the street, noticing his was not the only open carriage traveling towards the Park—which seemed ridiculous considering it was late February and still quite cold. He grunted. It would be slow going and crowded. Apparently, he was not the only one trying to make an impression today.

Normally, Hyde Park at the fashionable hour was the last place Jeremy would go. But he had made a decision, and this seemed the best way to go about it. Besides, if he waited, another gentleman might just beat him to it. He had discovered that Miss Pemberton was quite in demand at the ball last evening.

The door opened, and a footman looked out at him. Jeremy handed over his card. "I'm here to collect Miss Pemberton."

The footman motioned Jeremy inside. "Please wait—"

"I'm here, Marcus. There is no need to fetch me." She descended the staircase, and Jeremy's heartbeat ticked up. The reaction was not something he could explain. It was likely nerves. He had never done anything like this before.

There was something about this lady that intrigued him. The more he came to know her, the more he found to her advantage. He had observed that she still had moments of reserve but only around strangers. Besides some reserve was desirable, was it not? He grinned as he thought back to her conversation with Lady Derby. Her ability to talk her way out of trouble could be an asset in New Zealand. Indeed, if she weren't a woman, he might just advise her to seek a seat in Commons.

But it wasn't just that. She seemed to light up when they spoke of flowers or vegetables. What person became excited by a dinner course? He chuckled to himself. Her enjoyment of books would also prove useful at his new post, as there would be little entertainment.

But perhaps the most noticeable thing was what she did to him. Even Marlowe had remarked that Jeremy seemed happier— smiled more. It was something he had thought little about before, but it surely meant something.

Miss Pemberton gracefully descended the staircase, and Jeremy moved over to greet her. He bowed. "Miss Pemberton, you look very handsome today." His cheeks warmed. He had rarely said those words to a lady. His conversations were with sailors, and most of those were not suitable for the likes of Miss Pemberton.

Her smile faltered, and she reached up and touched her temple as she often did when someone paid her special attention. Her modesty was commendable.

He lifted his arm, and she tucked her hand into the crook. Jeremy missed a step. She had not simply put her hand *on* his arm. Rather, she held on, as if she wished for his support. It was a rather pleasant feeling.

Her father appeared from the corridor and leaned against the wall. His face was stern. "Jeremy, where are you taking my Nora?"

Miss Pemberton turned and looked over her shoulder at her father. "Papa, do you not remember? I told you at breakfast the Admiral had asked me to accompany him on a ride through Hyde Park this afternoon."

Her father winked at her. "Yes. I recall you mentioning the outing. But I like to instill a small amount of fear in any man escorting you." He raised a single brow at Jeremy. "I hope to scare them into treating my Nora as she deserves, if they had plans to do otherwise."

Jeremy might have been intimidated if he did not see the mischievous twinkle in the baron's eyes.

"Perhaps you'll join us for dinner this evening?" Lord Pemberton's face melted into a jovial smile.

Jeremy looked over at Miss Pemberton. Was she amiable to the invitation?

She nodded enthusiastically. "That would be lovely. Do say you will stay, Admiral."

Jeremy had expected the invitation to come once they had returned from the ride, but this would do nicely. He matched her enthusiasm and accepted.

Miss Pemberton tilted her head to the side, an amused look on her face.

"Is there something funny, Miss Pemberton?"

The color heightened in her cheeks, but she shook her head. "No, sir. I simply enjoy seeing you smile."

He didn't know how to respond, so he simply grinned wider and enjoyed the warmth spreading through his chest. Motioning to the door, he led her out and helped her up into the chaise. A sense of rightness settled over him as he jumped up and settled next to her. Soon they would arrive in Hyde Park, and everyone would see them. His chest puffed out slightly even as his hands sweat inside his gloves. He had battled Napoleon's Navy, yet it was Miss Pemberton sitting beside him that made him nervous.

His tiger handed up the reins and hurried to the back of the carriage, settling onto the small seat.

"You have a tiger?" Miss Pemberton glanced over her shoulder at the boy.

Jeremy shrugged. "Not because I need one. He was the son of one of my crewmen." A weight settled upon him whenever he spoke of the war. "He didn't survive. When the boy's mother fell ill, she sent him to me and asked if I might find him work. I could either employ him or send him to a workhouse. I just..." He shook his head.

She squeezed his arm. "You're a good man, Admiral."

Jeremy's brow furrowed. A better man would have seen that the boy never lost his father. But the past was the past, and he could not change it.

He flicked the reins, putting the chaise in motion.

"One day, when you're ready, I hope you'll tell me of your experiences at sea." Her voice was quiet next to him.

"There are few pleasant ones."

She shrugged. "I don't only wish to hear pleasantries, sir. I'm certain it was the unpleasant ones that taught you the most."

"Haunt me would be more accurate.

She scooted closer to him, wrapping both hands around his arm. A warm, orangey scent filled Jeremy's nose. It was a simple action, yet it lifted the weight nearly crushing him. She glanced over her shoulder. "You learned that boys need a father figure, not a workhouse. That is something."

He ducked his head. "You're giving me credit I don't deserve."

"I know you have faults, Admiral. We all do. But those faults do not diminish the good you have done."

He frowned. Now was not the time to dwell on the past. He

nodded to the line of carriages waiting to enter Hyde Park. "We will not be by ourselves today."

Miss Pemberton pulled her hands away, taking her warmth with her. She bundled her pelisse around her.

Jeremy reached under the bench and withdrew a rug. He set it on her lap. "Are you cold? Put this around your legs and it will keep you warm."

"Surely you are cold as well?" She held the rug over her lap and partially over his. She meant to share it? If he were being honest, he was not in the least bit cold. But he couldn't deny that the thought of sharing the blanket with her outweighed the heat pulsing through his skin.

He nodded his head, and she dropped half the blanket across his legs rather haphazardly. Jeremy transferred the reins into one hand, using his other hand to smooth it out. He glanced quickly at her.

"Thank you, I feel much warmer." Could she see he was lying? She obviously would when sweat beaded on his brow. Perhaps he would be lucky and a gust of wind would cool him down. Although that would likely just make her that much colder.

Jeremy steered the chaise through the gate into the park. The Ring was crowded with people and Rotten Row looked even more so.

He looked around, not fully understanding why so many of the *ton* enjoyed this activity. It was not as if there was any intimacy to be had. Indeed, with all the carriage noises and shouting going on, he didn't know how easy it would be to even carry on a conversation. He looked around them, trying to find somewhere he might speak with Miss Pemberton in relative quiet. This was obviously not the place to do it.

He frowned. The path was not yet nose to tail, but nor was there room to move the chaise faster than a crawl. Jeremy grunted. This was not how he had planned this afternoon.

Miss Pemberton, however, seemed content to lean back against the seat and watch everything around her. Her gaze moved from left to right, never settling on anything for longer than a moment.

He seemed to be the only one worried about the crowds. Perhaps he needed to change his disposition and simply enjoy the outing with her.

"Are you enjoying yourself, Miss Pemberton?" Jeremy asked.

"Yes, very much."

Jeremy transferred the reins to his other hand and placed his free hand on his knee. The chaise jolted as the wheel connected with a rut. His hand fell to the bench beside him.

Too late, he realized Miss Pemberton had grasped the edge of the bench to steady herself and now his hand grasped hers.

He bit the inside of his cheek, unable to look at their nearly clasped hands. Would she think he had done it on purpose? And if so, did she mind? Should he pull his hand away or would that only draw more attention to the action? Lud, the last time he had pulled away, she had become reserved and aloof. But this was different, was it not?

He breathed in slowly through his nose as he removed his hand, using the reins as an excuse. While he rather liked the feel of her hand beneath his, even if they both had gloves separating them, it was not time for such intimacies. However, if he could find an unoccupied area, things might just change in his favor.

A man on horseback stopped next to them. Mr. Blakemore tipped his hat to Miss Pemberton. "Good afternoon, Miss Pemberton."

She licked her lips, and her hand lifted to her curl. "Good afternoon, Mr. Blakemore." Her voice was quiet and reserved.

"What a surprise. Is it not too cold for you to be out in an open carriage?" Mr. Blakemore looked between the two of them, his gaze resting on Jeremy.

Miss Pemberton held up the rug. "The Admiral came prepared for the cold. I am quite comfortable."

Jeremy sat up a little taller. She likely was only referring to the blanket, but he wanted to think he had something to do with her comfort.

Mr. Blakemore's gaze flicked behind them. "I'm holding up the carriages. I'll bid you a good day, Miss Pemberton."

She nodded, but didn't smile. Why did that make Jeremy happy?

He frowned. What had come over him? He was not the sort of man to be jealous of another. Yet, there he was, wishing Mr. Blakemore away. But then he wished every person in the park away, so maybe it wasn't entirely jealousy.

A line of trees near the Grosvenor Gate looked promising. That lane seemed less crowded than the entrance at Hyde Park Corner. And while he could not see it from his vantage point, he thought perhaps the Cumberland Gate would prove even more secluded.

After stopping and starting over and over, Jeremy finally pulled the chaise to the side of the lane and turned in his seat to face Miss Pemberton. The breeze blew through the trees overhead, sending several crispy leaves fluttering to the ground. Reaching forward, he grasped her hands.

Her brows shot upward.

"Miss Pemberton, I've something I wish to speak with you about."

The tip of her tongue appeared between her lips, running slowly from one side to the other.

Jeremy's eyes followed the slow motion before the knicker of a horse pulled him back to the present. He pushed on. "It has been several days now since I—" A carriage rolled past them and Jeremy pulled back, releasing her hands. He watched as it rolled beyond them and turned toward Kensington Gardens.

"It has been several days..." Miss Pemberton prompted, bringing Jeremy's attention back to her.

"Er...yes. It has been several days since I decided—" He

stopped as a carriage approached from the other direction. Miss Pemberton's shoulders dropped and her lips pursed.

Drat, all these carriages! At this rate, it would be Easter before he finished the speech he had rehearsed all morning. "I have decided you would make a very fine wife."

"A wife?" Her brow creased.

"Yes. You have many qualities that make you exceptionally qualified. Especially for someone in my position."

She tilted her head to the side. "What qualities are these, per se?"

"You come from a fine family. They taught you proper etiquette. Watching you in Lady Derby's garden, I saw your diplomatic abilities."

"I have diplomatic abilities?" Her head tilted.

"Yes. And that kind of diplomacy could prove very helpful with the natives of New Zealand."

Miss Pemberton narrowed her eyes as if studying him. "You're comparing Lady Derby to the natives of New Zealand? I don't think she would appreciate it." She sighed. "Mother taught me how to behave in society, the same society as Lady Derby. She didn't teach me how to behave towards native peoples."

Jeremy raised a finger to cut her off. "Perhaps, but you're very observant. You'll discover how best to relate to the natives of New Zealand, just as you knew what to say to Lady Derby."

"How can you know I am observant?" She stared back at him.

One side of his lips quirked up. "I've noticed you watching me. That first night at dinner, you realized speaking of the war was hard for me and steered the conversation away." He looked down at his hands and cleared his throat. "Such skills could be useful."

She nodded. "As you have already said." She straightened on the bench. "Then you are asking me to marry you?"

"Yes, of course. Is that not what I said?" He frowned.

"You never actually asked, sir. You simply stated my advantages."

For someone who just received a proposal of marriage, she did not seem as happy as Jeremy had imagined.

What had he done wrong?

Chapter Nine

Admiral Fagan had asked her to marry him. Why was she not overjoyed? If the last year had taught her anything, it was that an offer of marriage was never guaranteed. Especially for someone in her situation. She was fortunate to have received one and from such an honorable gentleman.

Yet, she still found it difficult to be happy. Her dream had been to marry for love. There had been times over the last week when Nora had thought perhaps the Admiral might be developing affections for her, looks he gave her or small gestures—like placing his hand on hers only moments ago. Had that not meant something?

She twitched her lips to the side. Admiral Fagan had declared many things, but love was not among them. Gads, he made her sound more like a politician than a wife, which would not be so bad if not for her growing feelings for him. She would accept him without hesitation if he had offered her some words of love. But could she be happy in a marriage where she was the only one with such feelings?

Nora lifted a hand to the curl at her cheek. She had known the chances of her marrying for love were slim. And it was preposterous that she had allowed herself to believe it was still possible.

He was kind and treated her with respect. It was selfish, especially considering her situation, to want for more.

She pasted a smile on her face and turned toward him. "Admiral Fagan, I accept your offer."

He smiled widely, and her heart ached a little more. How had she thought such a look implied affection?

She swallowed down her disappointment. Perhaps he did not love her, but at least he found her agreeable. Many marriages could not boast that much.

"Excellent!" He sucked in a deep breath, almost as if he had been holding it while awaiting her answer. He took up the reins. "I'll speak to your father when we return."

"I'm certain he will not hesitate in giving you his blessing, Admiral."

He turned the chaise out of the park but glanced over at her. "I wish I had your confidence. Your father and I are friends, but I know he's fond of you, and it will pain him when you leave England."

Nora looked away. *Leave England . . . leave her family*. She had not considered that before accepting his offer. Could she leave England? How would she live without her family? Even if she didn't marry the Admiral, it was likely she would not live close to her parents. Many counties could separate them. But they would at least see each other at Christmastide or at a house party now and then.

But marrying the Admiral meant none of that would be possible. They would be separated by a vast sea, not just a few counties. And the separation would last for many years, even when his assignment in New Zealand finished. She pulled her bottom lip between her teeth. What had she done?

"We are engaged. I would not mind if you called me by my Christian name."

"What?" Surely in her wool-gathering she had misheard him.

"I think it entirely proper for you to call me Jeremy." He

wished for her to call him his Christian name? Should she tell him she had been thinking of him that way for days? Probably not.

She nodded. "If that's what you wish." She twisted at the finger of her glove.

"I would like it very much." He glanced quickly at her. "May I call you Nora?"

Her brow furrowed. Not ten minutes ago, she would have relished the idea. But now, things felt complicated and uncertain. It felt so intimate. "If that is what you wish," she said in a quiet voice.

Why could he not have said that he loved her? It would surely seem less daunting to leave her family if she knew he loved her. Knowing she would be leaving *all* her loved ones behind left her feeling rather bereft.

The Admiral—Jeremy—frowned. "Did I say something wrong?"

She shook her head. She could think upon all the implications later. Now she needed to stop making the situation worse than she had already made it. "No. Only my family calls me Nora. It simply took me by surprise."

"Would you prefer I call you something else?"

"No, please, Nora is fine."

His brow creased. "What about Hanora? Is that preferable?"

"Not Hanora." She blurted. "My mother only calls me that when she's angry with me." Her lips twitched. "When I was younger, I was called Hanora far too often."

He chuckled. "I find that both hard and easy to believe." He tapped his lips. "Perhaps I can come up with something better."

She raised a brow. "Something better than Nora?"

"Nora is lovely enough. But there is surely something more fitting. I simply need to figure it out."

The feeling of worry lifted slightly. If he was coming up with his own nickname for her, surely that meant something. Perhaps he was not in love with her now, but was it possible it would happen eventually? She touched her wig. Probably not unless a miracle happened and her hair grew back.

Her stomach lurched. *Her hair.* She should tell him about it. They were engaged, and he had the right to know. But would he cry off? Perhaps she need not worry about leaving England after all. She would discuss it with her mother later that afternoon.

He stopped the chaise in front of her home and helped her from the carriage. "I'll go speak to your father—if you're still amiable to the engagement?"

"Amiable? Of course, I am. You did nothing in the short drive back to change my mind."

He nodded and breathed in deeply. "Very good. I'll speak to your father then." He motioned her ahead of him.

Higgins opened the door and held it wide. "Welcome back, miss." He bowed to Jeremy. "Admiral."

"Is Lord Pemberton at home?" Jeremy asked.

"I'm at home for you, Jeremy." Lord Pemberton stepped into the entryway as if he had been waiting for their return. He walked over and kissed Nora on the temple. "The cool air was good for you, my dear."

She sighed. "Thank you, Papa."

"How was the park?" He asked.

Nora glanced at Jeremy and then back at her father. "It was lovely. A bit chilly at first, but the Admiral brought a very warm rug."

"I would expect nothing less from him." Her father clapped Jeremy on the shoulder and turned to him. "You wished to speak with me?"

"Yes, my lord."

"Let's retire to my study." He smiled at Nora. "Please excuse us, my dear."

Nora stared at their backs until they disappeared down the darkened corridor. When they returned from her father's study, it would be official. She would be engaged. If she had thought to change her mind, it was too late now. She would likely be married and on her way to New Zealand before spring fully emerged. The air left her lungs. Lawks, that was soon!

"Higgins, where is my mother?"

"She's in the North Parlor, miss."

"Thank you." Nora handed over her gloves and hurried away.

As she neared the parlor, she heard the strains of the pianoforte. Nora smiled and leaned against the wall, content to listen for a moment. Lizzie must be practicing. Several off notes sounded before the loud banging of a dozen keys at once.

"I'll never be proficient, Mama. I don't know why you continue to force me to practice."

Nora stepped into the room as Lizzie dramatically flung her arms onto the instrument and dropped her head down. "I prefer to paint, Mama. Why must you torture me?"

"You can't paint at a musicale, dearest. Now, try again, starting at the top of page two." Her mother looked up. "Ah, Nora. How was your ride with the Admiral?"

Nora stayed quiet for a moment. So many thoughts flitted about in her mind. Should she tell her mother or wait? What would her mother think? Would she be happy?

She should be. She had been pushing them together at every opportunity. But she wouldn't be happy about Nora leaving England.

Nora moved over to the piano, content to keep her news for a while longer. "Move over, Lizzie, and I'll play while you sing." She raised a brow at her mother. "Singing is a perfectly acceptable talent to perform at a musicale."

"Charlotte, my dear. Have you heard the news?" Lord Pemberton strode into the room with Jeremy right behind him. Nora dropped her hands from the piano and put them in her lap. Jeremy looked to be trying, unsuccessfully, to hide a smile. Her stomach fluttered, and she stood up quickly. This was it.

"What news, my dear?" Her mother asked.

"Jeremy has asked for Nora's hand, and she has accepted him." Her father looked at her with adoring eyes. He was truly happy about the union, but she could also see the worry lines creased at the side of his eyes.

Nora turned back, looking at her mother. How would she respond?

Her mother clapped her hands, jumping up from the couch. "Oh, Nora!" But then she became more solemn. "Oh, dearest. You'll be leaving us soon."

Nora swallowed as she nodded. The room stayed silent for several heartbeats.

Finally, her mother grasped her hands and spoke up. "Dearest, I'm so happy for you." She turned to Jeremy. "Admiral, I do hope you'll join us for dinner?"

Jeremy nodded. "Lord Pemberton already asked."

"Very good. I shall ask Cook to set another place. Is seven agreeable?"

"Indeed." He reached out and placed his hand on Nora's shoulder, giving it a gentle squeeze. "I shall take my leave for now. Until tonight."

"I'll see you out, Jeremy." Her father still smiled, but Nora could see an underlying sadness there.

Once the men left the room, Nora turned to her mother. "Mama, now that we are engaged do you not think I should tell him about my hair?"

Her mother's eyes widened. "Good heavens, child. Why should you think such a thing? There is no reason for you to tell him anything. By the time he discovers it, your problem will likely be over."

"Mama, how can you say that? There is no indication my hair will grow back. It is dishonest to keep such a thing from him."

"But will he not withdraw his proposal if he discovers it?" Lizzie stood up from the piano.

Her mother sighed. "Please, do be quiet, Lizzie. The Admiral is too much of a gentleman to cry off." She turned to Nora. "Has he shared everything with you? Do you know the details of his time at sea? What of his time in battle? He seemed very hesitant to share that information when I asked."

Nora shook her head. "No. There is much about that time that haunts him. But I don't see that it is the same."

"It is very much the same," her mother insisted. "Husbands and wives have their little secrets, dearest. Trust me."

Nora pulled her bottom lip between her teeth. "But what if I don't want to have secrets?"

"I'm not saying you should never tell him. I just think you should wait a little longer."

Nora slumped down onto the couch. "How much longer?"

Her mother patted Nora's leg. "Not long, dearest. I promise. When the time is right, you'll know."

How would she know? And what if Jeremy hated her once he discovered the truth? She would be truly alone then. And she didn't think she could survive that. It would be hard enough knowing her feelings for him were stronger than his for her, but if he should grow to hate her and her family lived an ocean away, it would be unbearable.

Besides, she knew she would feel deceived if the situation were reversed.

She nodded, even as she made up her mind. She did not care what her mother said. She would tell Jeremy the truth—and before the last bann was called. She just needed to find the right time.

Chapter Ten

Dinner, while pleasant, consisted mostly of questions and conversation between Jeremy and Lord and Lady Pemberton. Nora remained quiet, pushing her food about her plate. Even Miss Elizabeth had taken part in the conversation more than her sister.

Nora had not been rude, but Jeremy could not help but wonder if perhaps she was regretting her acceptance of his proposal. Or perhaps she was simply thinking. Much had happened today, and she likely needed time to figure it all out in her mind. He knew he certainly did.

Maybe he should have waited longer before he asked her, but Sir Thompson had been very pleased when Jeremy told him he was engaged. They may have only known each other for a few weeks, but they still had three more weeks to become better acquainted. And he knew enough to know they suited well.

But by the time they adjourned to the drawing room, Jeremy had almost convinced himself that Nora was only moments away from calling off the wedding. Dread settled in his stomach as they sat down in front of the fireplace. What would Sir Thompson do?

Hang Sir Thompson, what would Jeremy do? He had difficulty picturing his life without Nora in it. How had that happened in only a few weeks?

Lord Pemberton picked up the paper and Miss Elizabeth a book. Was this the normal way they entertained after dinner? Even Lady Pemberton seemed more concerned with her sampler than with Jeremy.

"Nora, why do you not play us a song on the pianoforte?" Lady Pemberton asked.

Nora hesitated.

"I would very much enjoy hearing you play." Jeremy adjusted his glasses on his nose. "And you *did* promise me."

"You see? The Admiral wishes to hear you also." Her mother motioned to the piano in the corner. "No one who has had the pleasure would turn down a second chance."

"Oh, Mama. You're doing it a bit brown." Nora rolled her eyes but stood up and looked down at Jeremy. "And you promised to sing." She smirked.

"Indeed, I did." He followed Nora, pulling over a second stool and placing it next to hers. He leaned closer to her and breathed in the citrus-y smell he'd enjoyed in the carriage. "I've been thinking," he whispered.

Her face pinked slightly. "About what?" Her voice was just as quiet as his.

"About what I shall call you."

She raised a pert brow. "Oh?"

"I think I've come up with the perfect name."

She spread sheets of music out but didn't look at him. "I can hardly contain my anticipation."

He grinned at her. This was the Nora he'd become accustomed to seeing of late, not the pensive lady from dinner. "I thought it should say something about you and your passions. My first thought was Carrot."

Her lips twitched. "You thought to name me after a vegetable?"

He shrugged. "You said they were your favorite to plant. I assumed you must like to eat them as well."

She nodded. "Indeed."

He stretched his arm behind the stool and gripped the edge, nearly encircling her with his arm. While he thoroughly enjoyed the feeling, it left him a bit at a loss for words.

She breathed in slowly. "You were saying about carrots?"

Jeremy shook his head, trying to regain the ability to think. "Yes, carrots. I thought perhaps it would suit, but when I look at you, I don't see carrots, so I discounted it."

Nora's lips twitched as she placed her fingers on the keys but didn't press down. "I think that's best."

"But then, the perfect name came to me."

She stared down at the keys. "Dare I ask? It's not lettuce, is it?"

He pointed to the music, as if he were speaking to her about it. He did not wish for Lady Pemberton to ask if something was wrong because it was taking them so long to begin. He tsked. "While that is lovely, I discounted it as well." He took in another breath of her. "No, I thought perhaps Daphne was better suited."

She turned to face him, and their noses nearly touched. The urge to kiss her was strong. Much stronger than when they had been in Lady Derby's garden. But he couldn't. What would her parents say? Lord Pemberton would likely throw Jeremy out on his ear.

She swallowed. "Daphne?"

He nodded. "Do you not like it? I thought they were perfectly lovely. A spark of color and vibrancy in a rather cold and colorless garden. They remind me of you."

A slow smile spread across her face, and for a moment he thought she might actually cry, which he was uncertain what to do about it. But the tears never came. Instead, she nodded. "I love it."

"Why are you not playing?" Her mother looked up from her sampler.

"The Admiral has agreed to sing along. We just need to decide on a song." Nora pulled out another piece. "What about this one, Admiral?"

Jeremy nodded, even though he was uncertain what the music was. He wished she would call him Jeremy. They were not at a society event, so would it not be acceptable?

"Oh, that is a surprise." Her mother gave them a mischievous smile.

"I know you said you don't play well, but I should love to hear you play something. What about this one?"

He shook his head. "Perhaps after you have played a few songs, I'll take a turn. By then your family will not be paying me any mind." He poked his finger at the page. "Come now, Daphne. I'm waiting to hear you play."

Her face lit up at the name, and Jeremy felt rather pleased with himself. It truly was the perfect name for her.

She had only played the first line of the music when he realized the truth of Lady Pemberton's words. Nora was a true proficient on the instrument.

"You may sing along any time now, Jeremy." She didn't whisper, but neither could her family hear her over the pianoforte. She had not called him Admiral.

He started singing quietly, so only she could hear. Nora grinned over at him. "You lied to me, sir. I hope it isn't to be a habit in our marriage."

"Lied? About what?" Jeremy's brow furrowed. They had only spoken of vegetables. How could he have lied about that?

"You said you were not a proficient singer."

Jeremy gave her a bland look. "That was not a lie, Daphne."

She shook her head. "I must disagree. You have a fine voice—one I should like to hear more often."

He held her gaze. "I'm certain it would only be enhanced if you joined me."

She clucked her tongue. "Very well, but I can assure you I am much more proficient on the pianoforte."

Her voice started out low and timid, but by the second line, it matched his in strength. Their voices blended in a way that surprised even Jeremy. His voice made hers sound better just as hers did for him.

The music stopped, and Jeremy stared at Nora as if they were under a spell. When he had proposed, he had told himself it was a practical decision—that she would be of benefit to him in his career. Which was true. But at that moment, it felt like more than practicality. It felt completely natural—as if they'd always been intended for each other.

His pulse thudded loudly in his ears.

Clapping slowly overpowered the noise in his head and pulled him from his thoughts. "You make a very fine duet," Lady Pemberton crooned.

"Thank you, Mama." Nora ducked her head.

"I believe it was your voice, Daphne, more than mine, that made the music lovely." He murmured.

She shook her head. "And I am certain it was you."

Lady Pemberton approached the pianoforte. "The two of you must perform together at Lady Holyoake's musicale next week." Excitement danced in her eyes.

Jeremy shook his head, his heart racing for a different reason. "I must decline the offer, my lady. I don't perform for the *ton*." He smiled down at Nora. "But I think you should."

Her eyes widened. "I cannot. There is nothing I dread more than performing at a musicale."

"But you perform so well together. Why should you not wish to do it?" Lady Pemberton pushed.

Nora looked down as one hand slowly came up to her temple.

"I believe you can do it." Jeremy straightened his glasses. "But what if we did it together, Daphne? That way, neither of us must do it alone?"

Nora looked up into his eyes. "Do you mean it?" her voice dropped to nearly a whisper.

He nodded. "I'll do it if you will."

She looked over at her mother. "Very well, Mama. We will perform one song together."

Nora and her mother shared a look, but Jeremy had no notion what it meant. "No one will find *anything* to criticize. Just you wait." Her mother returned to her seat on the couch and took up a stitchery from the nearby table.

Jeremy looked between mother and daughter. What had they communicated to each other without words? Would there ever come a time when he and Nora could do the same? A deep, intense longing settled in his chest.

He frowned. He had confessed no feelings of love when he had proposed. Indeed, he could not say if he felt such things for her. He enjoyed her company and found her very amiable. But love? He was not certain. He could not say what it felt like to be in love, as he had never experienced it. But neither had he ever felt as he did now.

Nora cleared her throat, drawing Jeremy out of his thoughts. "Could you turn the page, please?"

"I beg your pardon. I must have been wool-gathering." He turned the page of the music, but he didn't wish to abandon his thoughts altogether. There was something there that he had not identified yet.

The music stopped, and Nora placed her hand on his arm. "I've played for long enough. Would you play something for me?"

Jeremy grimaced. "After hearing you, I realize how poorly I play." While he did not think she would scoff at him, he didn't like feeling inadequate. "Really, I'm not proficient in the least."

Nora stood and moved next to the stool he was sitting on. "Jeremy, did you not just convince me to perform in the musicale? If I can do something that frightens me, I'm certain you can play when it is only family present."

Family. It had been a long time since he had been with family. He had not seen his oldest brother, the earl, in nearly a decade. Even his younger brother, Walter, who looked after Jeremy's estate, he rarely saw. They communicated through letters.

His crew was a sort of family, but it wasn't the same.

Jeremy scooted onto the other stool and Nora slid in beside him. She leaned across him, moving the music off the stand. His mouth went dry. No, he had never felt this way toward any member of his crew.

"Be brave, Admiral." She winked at him, and he realized how much he wanted this. How much he needed her in his life. How much he needed her *with* him.

"Very well. But remember, I warned you."

"Yes, and I choose not to heed your warning. Now pick your music and I shall turn the pages for you."

"Will you sing?"

She nodded.

Jeremy selected a rather simple piece, but it still proved difficult for him as he stumbled his way around the keyboard. Although how much of it was a lack of proficiency and how much was distraction every time she leaned over him to turn the page, he was uncertain.

"You see? I was completely truthful with you." He spoke with an I-told-you-so tone.

She lifted a shoulder and shook her head. "You're not as bad as you said."

"You are simply being kind, Daphne."

"Not kind, sir—simply truthful." She sighed and her lips slightly parted, drawing Jeremy's gaze down.

His pulse thudded in his neck, and he tugged at his cravat. "It has grown rather warm in here; do you not agree?" He stood up abruptly. Lord Pemberton would surely not agree with Jeremy's present thoughts.

Nora stood up, and they both walked toward the grouping of chairs where her family sat. She motioned to the footman standing at the door. "Charles, would you please ring for tea?"

Lord Pemberton put his paper to the side. "Tea. Capital idea, Nora."

Jeremy sat next to Nora on the couch. Neither spoke, but his eyes dropped often to her hand resting next to him. What would her parents say if he picked it up? They were engaged. Would it be so terrible?

He cleared his throat. "I've arranged for a box at the theater tomorrow next. Would you care to join me?" His gaze swept the group but came to rest on Nora.

"How fortuitous. It is the one evening we have free this week." Lady Pemberton cast a satisfied look at her daughter.

"Very good," Jeremy mumbled. "I shall call on you at six o'clock." He stood up and straightened his coat. "I should be on my way. Thank you for a lovely evening." He dipped his head, eager to feel the coolness of the night air on his skin.

Chapter Eleven

A t five minutes to six, Nora watched from her bedroom window as a carriage stopped in front of their town-house. Jeremy swung down to the walkway with more grace than Nora thought possible.

She squinted through the wavy glass at the man that was soon to be her husband. News of their engagement had spread faster than she had expected. At the Norcotts' card party last evening, it had been the main topic of conversation for the first thirty minutes. Several of the young ladies had given Nora appraising looks as if evaluating if she was worthy of Jeremy or not. She'd had to keep herself from twirling the curl around her finger—afraid that if she did, people would study her more intently and discover her secret.

She watched him until he disappeared under the portico and out of view.

Nora left her window seat and reached for the fan lying on her dressing table. She lifted a hand to her wig, ensuring it was properly placed.

"You look lovely, miss," Penny spoke from the corner of the room where she picked up the discarded chemise. "You need not worry about the wig. No one will be the wiser."

Nora nodded gratefully. "Thank you, Penny. You have been a blessing."

Penny ducked her head. She never had been one to accept praise. "Have a pleasant evening, miss."

Nora offered a little wave as she left the room. Once in the corridor, she paused and offered a prayer heavenward that nothing would go amiss. She didn't wish for Jeremy to learn about her hair because of a mishap. Perhaps she could invite him for tea tomorrow. She would feel far more comfortable giving him such news in the privacy of her own home.

Taking in a calming breath, she continued down the corridor but found herself halted again at the top of the staircase.

Jeremy stood in the entryway below, his hands clasped behind his back. His shoulders seemed broader than usual and his hair wavier. But that was likely because it was still wet— which was also why his gray side-whiskers looked more prominent. His gray-blue eyes sparkled in the chandelier's light.

Nora sighed. He was even more handsome than the first time she had seen him. There had been a moment while at the pianoforte the other evening when she had thought he might kiss her. The way he had looked at her—almost as if he could see into her soul. Then his gaze had dropped to her lips. Her breath halted even thinking about it. She had not known until that moment how much she wanted to be kissed. And not by just anyone. But by Jeremy.

In the end, no one had been kissed—a disappointing outcome from Nora's perspective. Instead, Jeremy had nearly jumped from the stool and spoke only of how warm it had become. She had chastised herself repeatedly for allowing herself to imagine him in love with her, even for a moment.

She placed a hand to her hair and pulled in a long, deep breath through her nose. It was just the theater. They would sit close to each other, but even with the chandeliers and candles, it would be darker than a ballroom or a parlor. Surely he would not notice the wig.

He looked up then, as if he could sense her watching him. His whole face smiled when he caught her gaze—making him even more handsome, if that were possible.

"Ah, Nora. There you are." Her father's voice boomed through the entryway. Had he been there the whole time?

Nora shook her head. She must focus more and spend less time wool-gathering.

"You look lovely, dearest." Her mother moved to Nora's side as soon as her feet touched the entry floor. Gracious, was everyone waiting on her?

"Thank you, Mama. You look lovely yourself." She glanced over and spotted Lizzie near the cloakroom door. "Lizzie, what a lovely gown." Her sister was certain to cause a stir when she came out next Season.

"Why do you two not go on ahead, and we will follow behind in our carriage?" Her mother feigned innocence.

"But there is plenty of room in my carriage," Jeremy protested.

"Yes, I'm certain there is, but poor Lizzie was complaining earlier of a stomachache—"

Lizzie looked confused and opened her mouth but shut it when her mother shot her a warning glance.

"I should be most distraught if we were all forced to leave early should it worsen."

Jeremy looked at Nora, a brow raised.

She shrugged. Her mother's plan was very transparent, not that she likely cared.

"Very well. We shall meet you there. Our box is accessible from the Bow Street entrance."

"Capital." Nora's father looked pleased.

Jeremy held out his arm, and Nora took hold of it. "This way, Daphne," he murmured close to her ear. Gooseflesh erupted on her skin.

He helped her into the carriage and swung up behind her, settling in on the seat opposite.

Nora smirked. That was surely not what her mother had in mind when she suggested the second carriage. But the smirk died away when Nora realized it was not what she'd had in mind, either. Why would he not sit next to her?

He cleared his throat. "Your mother and I are in agreement. You look very handsome this evening."

Nora's face heated. The pale green gown brought out the green flecks in her amber eyes. It was one of the reasons she had selected it at the modiste's, hoping people would look more closely at her eyes rather than her hair.

"Thank you." She looked out the window at the fading light. Even now, men walked along the street, lighting the lamps.

Silence hung between them as if neither knew what to say to the other.

Unable to abide the silence any longer, she spoke up. "Have you been to the theater since coming to London?"

He shook his head and pushed his glasses up. "No. Your father volunteered *you* to accompany me. I could not in good conscience go without you."

Ah, their easy banter was back. Nora released a heavy breath. "Volunteered? It was more like he insisted you invite me." She shook her head. "I should apologize for him."

"You need not apologize." Jeremy chuckled. "I like to believe I would have invited you anyway—without your father's involvement."

"Oh? Would you have?"

Jeremy nodded, a look of feigned insult on his face. "I'm not afraid of your father, Daphne. I invited you to take the turn around St. James Square of my own accord. The same is true of our drive in Hyde Park. Your father had nothing to do with my decisions."

"Then you would have come to those ideas even if my father had not mentioned taking me to the theater?"

He nodded.

"Why?"

His head stilled, and he stared at her. "Why? Why what?"

"Why would you have asked me without his prompting?" She did not know why she was pressing the issue; it really didn't matter. Except it did. She needed to know what exactly he liked about her.

She bit the side of her cheek. *Please don't say it was because I'm handsome.*

"At first it was, perhaps, because I knew your family." He looked down at his trousers. "Your father has been an important man in my life."

"And after?"

He held up his hand. "Patience, Daphne." He stood up, or as much as one could in a carriage, and moved next to her. "The lady I met in the entry hall when I first came to London seemed so different from what I thought I needed—" he cleared his throat. "What I thought I wanted."

"Which changed? The girl in the entryway or what you wanted?"

He lifted a shoulder. "Perhaps a little of both. As I came to know the lady from the entryway, I realized she was not who I thought she was."

Nora's scalp suddenly itched terribly, and she lifted a hand. But there was no way to satisfy it without shifting the wig. He *thought* he knew her "It sounds as if she's what changed." Nora twisted at her fingertips, trying to keep her mind off the itch.

"No. What I wanted also changed. Perhaps it was because of what I discovered that made me realize what I truly wanted."

"And what did you discover?" The itch moved down her body to her throat.

"I discovered a lady with grace and intelligence and a depth of character but bearing a carefree spirit about her." He ran his hands down his thighs. "I envied that carefree spirit. But I realized when I was with her, she helped free that part of me I didn't know existed."

The tips of her fingers tingled.

He had not mentioned her beauty. Several years before, such an omission would have offended her. But now she was more grateful than she could ever put into words. "Thank you. I don't believe anyone has ever said anything so kind."

He smiled. "Besides, any gentleman would be pleased to have such a handsome young lady on his arm."

Thunder and turf! Nora swallowed. Why had he ruined it?

The carriage came to a stop, and Nora had never felt so relieved. She needed to breathe in the cold air—feel it burn her throat and lungs. Surely that pain could push aside the pain in her chest. If she could just tell him the truth.... Although, once he learned of her secret, a different pain would certainly replace it.

She looked out the window. They were not in front of the Theatre Royal, Covent Garden, as she expected, but several streets away.

Jeremy frowned. "I figured this would be the way of it. We must either wait for the carriages ahead to empty, or we must disembark here and walk the rest of the way."

Nora couldn't stay in the carriage for another moment. "Let's walk. The carriage has become rather stifling. Do you not agree?" She stood up, and Jeremy jumped at her abruptness.

"Of course. If that's what you wish." He hurried and knocked on the door before throwing it open and stepping out.

Nora sighed. *What she wished?* She wished he had never mentioned her beauty. Did he not understand that beauty was only temporary? Yes, her mother was still a handsome woman for her age. But she was nothing to the beauty she had been when she was as young as Nora. And as Nora could attest, not even the young could count on their beauty to remain for long. Things happened. Accidents happened. And sometimes, hair fell out and left a person bald and ugly.

Chapter Twelve

Jeremy lifted his arm, and Nora tucked her hand into the crook. He placed his other hand atop hers. This was how things should be.

A gust of wind blew through an alley, nearly toppling Jeremy's beaver. He quickly grabbed hold and pushed it firmly down on his brow. "Are you warm enough?"

She nodded.

"Did you enjoy Lady Norcott's card party last evening?"

Nora shrugged. "I'm not overly fond of cards. But Mama enjoys playing Hearts." She held on to him with both hands when she came to a large puddle. Jeremy led her carefully around, and they continued on.

Nora looked up at him. "It surprised me you were not there."

He grimaced. "I had already accepted an invitation to Admiral Crawford's card party. Although, I'm certain I should have enjoyed my time better with you at Lady Norcott's." He glanced sidelong at her. "The company would have been far better."

She smiled sweetly but did not reply.

When they finally reached the theatre, both breathed out puffs of warm air. "Here we are." Jeremy led her through the doors into the vestibule and up the stairs.

Their box was empty, leaving them their pick of seats. Jeremy moved toward the front row, but Nora reached out a hand to stop him. "Do you mind if we take the seats in the back?"

He shook his head. "We may sit wherever you like. But it will be more difficult to see the stage."

Nora lifted a shoulder. "I should prefer the lesser view so as not to be on display for everyone else."

Did she not wish to be seen with him? He pushed the thought down. He knew Nora. She didn't wish for attention from others any more than he did. It should not surprise him that she wished to sit in the back.

His gaze dropped to her lips. There could be other advantages as well. He sighed. While he had dreamed of kissing her more than once the previous night, he did not believe Lord Pemberton would be any more amiable to it tonight than he had been two nights ago.

She sat down next to the thin wall dividing one box from the next and looked toward the stage. "The view from here isn't so bad. I think we shall still see the actors."

He sat down next to her and crossed his legs, his foot knocking into the chair in front of him. The chairs were deuced uncomfortable and so close together. How did people sit in them for hours on end?

She leaned forward in her seat, stretching her neck and twisting her head to see the details of the building.

"We may move to the front seats if you like." It was not as if he would steal a kiss no matter which row they sat in.

Nora shook her head. "No. This will do."

The theatre continued to fill with people, and the play finally began.

"Where are my parents and Lizzie?" Nora looked around them as if she thought her family had simply sat in the wrong box. "You don't think something happened to them, do you? What if there was an accident?"

Jeremy tilted his head. "They are likely caught in the line of carriages—if they ever left at all," he muttered low. He could easily see Lord and Lady Pemberton staying away on purpose to give Nora and him a chance to be alone. Now that they were engaged, there was no need for a chaperone. He rolled his eyes at the ridiculousness of it. How were they to be alone with thousands of people surrounding them?

He looked around their empty box. If Lord and Lady Pemberton wished for Jeremy and Nora to be alone, surely Lord Pemberton would not oppose Jeremy kissing Nora.

They had tucked themselves into a corner, nearly completely in the dark and mostly hidden from the view of those in the other boxes.

Maybe they were more alone than he previously believed. He picked up her hand and gave it a squeeze, glancing over at her from the corner of his eyes to see if she disliked the contact.

She stared at the stage as if nothing had happened.

He raised a brow. Just what would it take to ruffle the unruffleable Daphne?

He stared at the stage as he pulled her hand over and rested it on his thigh. Her eyes widened, and Jeremy held back the smile. It was a reaction but not a grand one. He must try harder.

He placed his palm atop hers and slowly dragged his thumb from the bottom of her hand to the tip of her thumb. Back and forth he swept and with every sweep he felt her give a tiny shudder. But was it a good shudder or a bad one? He had to admit; he was not well-versed in shudders.

He stopped the movement, and her shoulders dropped a fraction. She thought he was done. Jeremy chuckled to himself. Not by a long way.

He entwined their fingers and placed their connected hands into his empty one, encasing her small hand in his. She stared unblinking at the stage. Was she willing him to push further?

Leaning into her, he whispered. "Are you enjoying Miss Eliza O'Neill's performance?" He could just make out the curve of her neck in the small amount of light from the chandelier. The hairs on the back of her neck swayed with his every word and her shoulders lifted with shallow breaths.

Jeremy grinned in triumph when she swallowed. She was not as unaffected as she let on.

He breathed in deeply, planning to tickle her neck with one last exhale. The soft scent of orange and vanilla tickled his nose, stopping him in his tracks. It was intoxicating.

"Her performance is even better than I had heard." Nora turned toward him, and it was no longer her neck he stared at. Her soft lips parted, and Jeremy could not think about anything but holding her in his arms and kissing her as he had in his dreams.

Closing the slight distance between them, he paused a moment before his lips captured hers. Did she want this as much as he did? He would not continue if she showed any hesitation.

She leaned forward, pressing her lips to his. It was all the invitation he needed. He lifted his hand and cupped her cheek. Pulling her closer, he kissed her more fully, rubbing his thumb softly along her jawline.

His other hand dropped from her face and cradled her neck at the hairline. What would it feel like to plunge his fingers into her curls?

Nora jerked away from him. And he leaned back in his chair, breathless. Why had she pulled away?

She looked anxiously out at the crowd and then at him. Worry hovered in her eyes. Had he taken the kiss too far? Did she worry others may have seen them?

The crowd erupted into applause. The play had stopped for intermission. And so, it seemed, had the kissing.

She turned back toward him, her fingers lightly caressing her lips. The worry lines deepened around her eyes as she lifted a trembling hand to her hair.

Jeremy straightened in his seat. "Lud, Daphne. I'm sorry." Why had he not controlled himself? It was most unlike him.

A pain seared through his chest. How could he have hurt someone he loved so recklessly?

He paused, and the air whooshed out of him. *Love.* There was no question in his mind. He knew, without a doubt, that he loved Nora. He wanted to tell her right then and there, but he worried she would think it was simply a response to the kiss. Would she believe he was sincere? But more than that, what if she didn't love him in return?

Chapter Thirteen

Nora shifted the pearl-lined ribbon encircling her head. She didn't like wearing tiaras or ribbons in her hair. The extra weight made her wig feel off-kilter, shifting from one side to the other. It was only slight, but she still felt the constant need to adjust it.

Nora dropped her head to the side. "Mama, will you be sad when I leave with Admiral Fagan? I'll not see you for many years."

Her mother's lip quivered. "How could you ask such a thing?" She paused, wringing her hands in front of her. "Of course I'll be sad, but I also could not be happier for you. The Admiral is a good man. I know he'll see you're taken care of." She swallowed. "And when he has retired, you may return to England to your own estate. There will be difficulties ahead of you, that's certain." She lifted a hand and placed it on Nora's cheek. "But you'll handle it with grace and competence. Just as you always do."

Nora's vision blurred. "Thank you, Mama. I'll miss you desperately."

"Ah, you are both ready and looking as handsome as ever." Her father bounded into the entryway. "Jeremy sent word that he'll meet us at the musicale."

Nora sagged. She had been looking forward to riding in the carriage with him. After their kiss last evening, neither had said much the rest of the evening. But after sleeping—or not sleeping—she was eager to see him again.

Did he still feel the same way, or had last night simply been the magic of the theater? She reached up to her wig and ran her hand lightly over the knot. Why had she not told him yet? The longer she waited, the more difficult it became. Perhaps, if they found a quiet moment together, she might find the courage. She shook her head. No, she *must* find the courage to tell him.

"Come along. We don't wish to be late." Her father shooed them toward the door and their waiting carriage.

THE HOLYOAKES' townhouse was brightly lit by a large, ornate chandelier in the entryway. A footman took their cloaks and disappeared.

"Please follow me." The butler led them down a corridor and motioned them into a large room with a pianoforte front and center. People milled about, talking and laughing. A table at the far end held three large bowls of bright, yellow lemonade.

Her mother lifted a hand in a wave and hurried off to visit with Mrs. Pendrake.

Nora looked about the room, searching for only one person.

"Good evening, Miss Pemberton." Mr. Blakemore sidled up beside her.

Lud, not him. "Good evening," Nora smiled but continued to scan the room.

Mr. Blakemore sighed. "Ah, there is Mr. Jeffers. Please excuse me."

Nora could not feel bad for her poor behavior. She would not be long in this society, so what did it matter if she offended the likes of Mr. Blakemore?

"Are you thirsty? Shall I fetch us both some refreshment?"

Jeremy's low voice sounded just behind her, his breath tickling her neck.

She turned, her heart jumping into her throat. "Jeremy, I was just looking for you."

He looked down at her, and his eyes twinkled. "And now you have found me."

All her earlier concerns over his feelings fled. Could he look at her in such a way—kiss her with such passion—if he did not care about her? It didn't seem possible. But would he feel the same passion when he discovered her secret?

She shook the unwanted doubts away. For now she would enjoy the musicale and worry about the rest when the proper time presented itself.

Jeremy lifted his arm, and she took it. He led her over to the refreshment table and presented her with a glass of lemonade.

"I'm sorry I could not accompany you. My meeting with Sir Thompson went longer than expected."

"Is he not the man who assigned you to your new post?"

Jeremy nodded. "Yes. We were discussing some of the finer details of the mission." His smile widened. "He wondered if you might help me purchase gifts to take with us. We think it wise to take some for the women. They may prove to be an ally in convincing the men of our friendly intentions."

She looked at him. "And you believe gifts will earn their respect and friendship?"

Jeremy shrugged. "Not wholly."

"Then why take them?"

"The gifts are a starting point. I'll only earn their trust by showing them kindness and respect. No gift can overcome the brutality and disrespect shown them in the past." He sighed. "I fear we will have an uphill battle."

She sipped her lemonade and puckered at its tartness. "I thought you said no one had colonized there."

"No one has. Various expeditions have spent time on the

islands, charting and mapping the area. Those from the expeditions did not always behave as Englishmen ought."

Nora smiled up at him. Every new thing she learned about him only convinced her she had done well in her choice of a husband. "They have selected the right person for the job. I've never known a better man."

He lifted a hand, as though he were going to cup her cheek or touch her hair, but then he glanced around him and dropped it back down. "Thank you, Daphne," he whispered. He straightened up and looked seriously at her. "Are you certain you wish to make this journey, Nora? We did not discuss that aspect of our engagement."

She might have doubted his intentions if she had not seen the look of admiration and—dare she believe—love in his gaze. She nodded. "I'm certain."

He opened his mouth, but Lady Holyoake clapped her hands, cutting him off. "Everyone, please be seated. We shall begin our musicale in mere moments."

Jeremy cupped Nora's elbow in his hand and led her over to the seats next to her mother. Her father had likely taken refuge in the card room. Her mother smiled up at them. "Good evening, Admiral."

Jeremy helped Nora into her seat and settled in next to her. "Please, Lady Pemberton. We are to be family. I insist you call me Jeremy."

"Jeremy," she tittered. "The two of you will be the last performance before intermission." She fluttered her fan. "You'll be the talk of the musicale; I just know it."

Lady Holyoake announced the first number, and a lovely young girl made her way to the front to play the pianoforte.

"I'm already nervous." Nora scooted closer to him, his warmth helping to calm her.

"You need not be nervous, Daphne. You'll perform masterfully." Jeremy picked up her hand as he had the night before. Tingles traveled up her arm and through her body at his touch. He laid her hand in his, lightly tracing each of her fingers.

Nora nearly pulled her hand away, not because she didn't like it, but because she liked it too much. She thought of nothing but Jeremy and his kisses while he played with her fingers.

It was the applause that finally pulled her out of her reverie. Blinking several times, she tried to clear her head. She reluctantly pulled her hand from Jeremy's and clapped, even though she had no notion if the performance was worthy or not.

He leaned over and she both hoped that he would and prayed that he wouldn't kiss her again. "I'm looking forward to intermission," he whispered.

She smiled nervously. "Oh? Why is that?"

His gaze dropped to her lips. "It has been nearly twenty-four hours since last I kissed you. I don't know that I can wait another hour to do so again."

She let out a shaky laugh as the next performer moved to the front of the room. This was not the man she had met in their entryway several weeks ago. But she could not say she disliked the change.

He pulled her hand back to his and started his sweeping motion again. Gads, she could not take this for the whole evening. It would drive her mad. She pulled her hand away, clasping it in her lap.

Jeremy raised a brow, and she shook her head at him in feigned irritation.

That was how it went for every performance. He would take her hand; she would pull it back. It became a sort of game to see who could keep her hand the longest. By the time intermission approached, Jeremy was ahead. It became harder and harder to pull her hand away from him when all she wanted was to feel his touch.

Lady Holyoake stood. "We have one last performance before we take a brief intermission and allow everyone some refreshment." She looked out into the seated crowd. "Ah, Miss Pemberton. There you are."

Nora stood up and pulled Jeremy up beside her. "Do not think you're abandoning me now," she muttered under her breath.

"I wouldn't dream of it, Daphne." He followed her closely down the aisle and took a seat next to her at the pianoforte. "Just pretend it is you and I singing in your parents' parlor."

Nora placed shaking hands on the keyboard. She looked him in the eyes, and all the tension flowed out of her. She could do anything if he was beside her. Pressing the keys down, she played.

Jeremy's rich voice filled her ears, and Nora blocked out everyone else in the room.

At the end of the song, she lifted her hands from the keyboard and waited for the instrument to quiet down. She didn't dare look out into the audience. But she need not wait long for their reaction. Applause filled the room. They both stood and moved away from the piano. The clapping died down and the rest of the crowd joined them in the aisles.

Jeremy clasped Nora's hand and lifted it to his lips. "You were amazing."

She laughed giddily. "It was not just me." She took a step closer to him, leaving little space between them. "I don't know how to thank you, Jeremy. I could never have done it without your help."

He grinned wickedly. "I have an idea how you can thank me." He waggled his brows and pulled her along behind him.

Nora giggled ridiculously as she tried to keep up with his long stride. Her stomach fluttered like a flock of birds—all of them taking flight at once.

Jeremy stepped into the corridor and looked in both directions. "I think this way should provide us with some privacy."

Her nerves tingled. She had performed and survived the experience. There was little she could not do at that moment, but there was only one thing she wished to do. And that was to kiss the man tugging her down the dimly lit corridor.

They turned several corners and Nora felt confident she would never find her way back without help. Hopefully Jeremy knew where they were going.

They reached the end of a corridor, and Jeremy twirled her around, sliding his hands around her waist. "I think this is private enough."

He moved her back against the wall and lowered his head toward her. "It was deuced difficult paying attention to Sir Thompson when all I wanted to do was see you."

They must have been deep within the house because Nora could no longer hear the chatter of voices over the thudding in her ears. The only light came from the moon, shining through a window and a few sconces dotting the wall.

All she wanted to do was kiss him, but she knew she needed to tell him the truth first. It might deny her his kiss one last time, but perhaps that was for the best. The more he kissed her, the more she would miss it when it was gone.

She looked up at him and swallowed. "Jer—" His lips found hers before she could finish his name. The kiss was even better than the first. His mouth explored hers as he'd not been able to before because of the position of the chairs. But nothing stood in his way here.

Her mind emptied of all its thoughts, and she clutched at his lapels, never wanting the moment to end.

Much too soon, Jeremy pulled back, breathing hard. He dropped his forehead to hers and sighed. "Lud, Daphne. What have you done to me? I used to be such a levelheaded man, but you have me escaping into darkened corridors just to steal a kiss from you." He raised a hand and gently ran a finger over her lips, across her jaw, and down her neck. "But I suppose it is love I should blame, not you."

She looked up at him, and her mouth parted. "What?" She had longed to hear him say those words.

He nodded. "It's true. I love you. When I asked for your hand, I didn't realize how much I cared for you. Indeed, I likely already loved you and was just too daft to realize it."

Nora reached up and smoothed the creases next to his eye. She loved those creases. "I love you too, Jeremy."

He leaned in and kissed her again. Where the first had been crushing and passionate, this one was soft and tender, nearly taking her breath away.

"Nora, Jeremy, is that you? The intermission is over."

Nora pushed Jeremy away at the sound of her father's voice. Gads, why did she feel so guilty when she had done nothing wrong? She ran her fingers over her pulsing lips. Perhaps not entirely nothing.

"Papa." Nora moved to step around Jeremy and the compromising position when she felt her wig shift. She lifted a hand, but it was too late. Before she could stop it, the wig came free, and the stolen kiss was the last thing on her mind.

Nora gasped and grabbed the wig hanging limply from a curl at the bottom of the wall sconce.

She turned to see the gape-mouthed faces of Jeremy and her father.

Unable to speak a word, she fled down the corridor, trying to pull the wig back into place as she tried to find her way out of the Holyoakes' townhouse.

Chapter Fourteen

"Please, do hurry, Marlowe. I must see Miss Pemberton immediately, and I've a stop to make on my way." Jeremy had tried going after Nora following the mishap the previous evening, but Lord Pemberton had insisted she needed time.

Jeremy had given her fourteen hours. He glanced at the clock. And thirty-two minutes. He could not afford a minute longer. He wanted to see her—needed to see her.

Marlowe raised a brow. "It is a trifle early for a social call, sir."

"I'm aware. But I can't wait any longer."

Marlowe tied the last knot in Jeremy's cravat and helped him into his waistcoat and tailcoat.

When he reached for the brush, Jeremy shook his head. "I have no time for that this morning." He shrugged his shoulders, settling his coat in place. "Wish me luck, Marlowe. I must fix this. I can't leave for New Zealand without Miss Pemberton at my side."

"Do you have a departure date?"

"Sir Thompson wishes me to leave soon after the wedding." He shook his head. "But I don't know what will happen if there is no wedding." He rubbed at the ache in his chest. What if she didn't take him back?

"Good luck, sir." Marlowe dropped the brush onto the dressing table and stepped aside.

Jeremy plucked up his hat and greatcoat from the chair near the door and took the stairs two at a time. He hoped Mr. Mercer's apothecary was open at this hour. If not, he would have to inquire at the man's apartment.

Stepping outside, he breathed in deeply and offered a little prayer that things would fall in his favor today.

LORD PEMBERTON WALKED with Jeremy to the sitting room.

Nora turned to glance at him as he stepped inside. He didn't know if she had heard him or simply sensed his presence.

He sighed at the sight of her.

"Admiral Fagan, I expected to receive a missive, not the man himself." She looked out the window, keeping her back to him. A mobcap had replaced her wig.

"Ours is a face-to-face conversation. There are many things the written word cannot convey, and I don't wish for there to be any misinterpretation."

Nora shifted but did not turn around. "I can assure you, there is nothing to misinterpret. You need not have come. I release you from our engagement."

"That is most kind of you, Daphne," he said in a dull tone. "But do I not have a say in the matter?"

"What's there to say?" Her voice held a note of defeat.

"That you love me?" Jeremy let out a ragged breath and ran his fingers through his hair. "Nora, may we please sit down? I should like to look upon you when we speak."

A mirthless laugh sounded. "I doubt that, sir."

He clenched his fists at his side. "Please?" He was not above begging.

Her shoulders rose on a breath but then returned to their hunched position. "Very well. If that's what it will take for you to leave."

His jaw worked furiously.

She sat on the edge of the settee and tugged at the edge of her mobcap. She looked at the package in his hands and then up at his face.

Was it a good idea to give it to her? At the time he had purchased it, he had thought it was nothing short of genius. But now he was second-guessing his decision.

She stared at the package expectantly.

He held it out, holding his breath when she took it. "This is for you, although perhaps I should explain—"

She pulled the string, and the paper fell away, revealing the apothecary's label on the pouch. She looked at him with raised brows. "This is for hair re-growth." It was a simple sentence, yet her tone told far more than her words.

Gads, the package had been a bad idea. "I thought you may appreciate it. The apothecary—he is a friend of mine—discovered this remedy while he was traveling in South America."

She set the pouch aside. "What a *thoughtful* gift."

Jeremy sighed. "I purchased it because you seemed distraught over..." He glanced at her mobcap.

Her gaze dropped to the floor. And he knew it had not been the correct thing to say.

She held the package out to him. "I think it best if you left." Seeing her so devoid of all joy pierced his heart.

Jeremy held up his hand. "Please, I meant no offense. Use the powders or don't. It is up to you. I could not care one wit."

"Yes, I should think you do not. You're released from our engagement. What does it matter to you?"

"Why must you keep saying that? I'm not the one pushing me away."

Her mouth opened and then snapped shut. Her brow furrowed as she processed his words. "Why would you not wish to be released? I lied to you about something very important."

"Perhaps your lack of hair—" She flinched and he grimaced. Why did everything he say sound so horribly wrong?

He started again. "Your *situation* may have been important if it was the reason I asked for your hand. But it wasn't." He scooted closer to her on the settee, wanting to reach for her hand but uncertain if it would cause more problems. "Daphne, you are so much more than your hair." He lifted his hand and touched her cheek. "I love you just as you are."

"A lie can go a long way if you look as though it is the truth." She quoted his words from Lady Derby's garden back to him and held up the package. "If you don't care about my hair, why did you bring me this?"

He scrubbed his hand over his face and grunted. "You seemed so upset when your wig pulled free last evening." Indeed, he could not close his eyes without seeing the horror on her face. "I've noticed the way you touch your temple when you're feeling vulnerable. If hair will make you feel more at ease, I want you to have it. But if you use the powders, do so for yourself. Not because you believe I, or anyone else, will think better of you."

She looked down at the pouch and fingered the label. "I'm sorry I did not tell you. It must have been a terrible shock for you. I meant to tell you—" She glanced up, tears pooling in her lids. "I was just so afraid."

"Afraid I would reject you." He closed the distance between them and took her hands in his. "I love you, Daphne, with or without hair. Please don't send me away. Say you will marry me, and let me prove my love to you every day."

"What if this does not work?" She looked at the powders.

"My feelings will not change."

She sighed. "But society will not be so accepting."

He lifted a hand and wiped a tear from her cheek. "We will try different powders. Or I'll buy you the best wig in London. Lud, I'll buy you a dozen wigs, if that will make you happy."

Nora pulled her hands from his and wiped at a tear with the back of her hand.

She took in a shuddering breath. "I'm sorry for doubting you, Jeremy." She leaned in and flung her arms around his neck. "Thank you," she whispered in his ear.

"It is I who should thank you." He tried to pull back, but she buried her face in his neck and shook her head.

"No. I need to thank you for loving me, just as I am."

Author's Notes

Thank you for reading Just as You Are.

I loved writing this story. This is my version of the fairytale The Ugly Duckling. I have always liked this story because I think it is one that does not lose its relevance. Indeed, I think it is as relevant today as it ever has been. We live in a world where it is hard not to place our value on how others see us outwardly. But this fairytale shows us that we all have massive potential to grow into something amazing. Even if it does not show on the outside.

Alopecia is not a new disease. In fact, the term dates to the mid-1600s. Although, in those days, they did not fully understand the cause of the disease. It may not have been as devastating of a problem in earlier centuries, especially among the upper classes because wigs were commonly worn and considered high fashion. Hygiene at the time was such that lice were very common, and people often shaved their heads in order to keep the infestations minimal.

However, by the late eighteenth century and into the nineteenth century, wigs fell out of fashion and natural hair was in style. At this time, Alopecia would have been a very tragic thing to have happen to a person. Especially to an upper-class young lady who has not yet married.

While I know that everyone reacts differently to trials and hardships, I tried to make Nora's feelings and reactions honest and relatable. I know that many people place a high value on their outward appearance, and the Regency period was no different.

However, I did not want this story to be sad and depressing. I wanted to show that even with the bad, there can be some good. And that good came in the form of Jeremy. Not that I believe that we should get our self-worth from others. But I think sometimes it takes someone else to help us see that there is more to us than just the person we see in the mirror or the well-cleaned glass. I hope I was able to convey that in this story.

I hope you enjoyed Nora and Jeremy's story. I enjoyed writing it so much that I may just write some more fairytale retellings. Stay tuned!

Acknowledgments

A huge thank you-

To my editors Cara Seger and Brandalyn Seaman for fixing all my plot holes and poor grammar—because I know it is there.

To my proofreaders: Patti Knowlton and Rose Hutchison for catching all those pesky typos that seem to slip through.

To my great writers' group: Laura Beers and Laura Rollins! Thanks for all the help you give me to tighten my storyline and help me improve on my ideas! You guys are the best!

To my great ARC team. Thank you for all you do to help me be successful! I couldn't do it without you guys.

And last and most importantly, to all my boys—big and small. Thanks for not complaining when you were out of clean clothes or get pizza for dinner...again. For reading over my shoulder and telling me you thought my story sounded 'really good.' And for encouraging me—telling me I 'made a good job choice to become an author.' I love you, tons! Especially to Christopher for supporting and helping me push through when it just felt too hard and for making sure I had the tools I needed to make me successful. You are my great cheerleader! I couldn't do this without your support! LY

Also By

Regency House Party Series

Mistaken Identity

Miss Marleigh's Pirate Lord

Scoundrels, Rakes and Rogues Series

Reforming the Gambler

Rake on the Run

The Secrets of a Scoundrel

Unlikely Match Series

An American in Dukes Clothing

The Baron's Rose

A Princess for the Gentleman

Bells of Christmas Series

Unmasking Lady Caroline

Thawing the Viscount's Heart

Hidden Riches Series

The Mysteries of Hawthorn Hall

The Treasure of Owl's Roast Abbey

League of Eligible Bachelors

Engaging the Earl

Top Flight Series

Bear: A Fighter Pilot Romance

Mustang: A Fighter Pilot Romance

Want more? Sign up for Mindy's newsletter here to receive updates, deals, and new releases.

About the Author

Mindy loves all things history and love, which makes writing romance right up her alley. Since she was a little girl playing in her closet "elevator," she has always had stories running through her mind. But it wasn't until she was well into adulthood that she realized she could write those stories down.

Now they occupy her dreams and most every quiet moment she has.

Her kids are used to being called names they have never heard and they now use words like vexed and chagrined.

When she isn't living in her alternate realities, she is married to her real-life Mr. Darcy and trying to raise five proper boys. They live happily in the beautiful mountains of Utah.

You can connect with her on her website mindyburbidgestrunk.com.